SURVIVAL BY MAGIC

SURVIVAL BY MAGIC

THE SARIAH CHRONICLES™ BOOK THREE

PETER GLENN

MICHAEL ANDERLE

THE SURVIVAL BY MAGIC TEAM

Thanks to our Beta Readers
Larry Omans, Kelly O'Donnell, Allan Collins

Thanks to our JIT Readers

Diane L. Smith
Veronica Stephan-Miller
Dorothy Lloyd
Deb Mader
Angel LaVey
Kerry Mortimer

Editor

SkyHunter Editing Team

CHAPTER ONE

"Well, *Scheisse*," Harvey said. He looked up at the sky. Fresh clouds were forming overhead.

It would rain again soon.

His eyes drifted back to Sariah. "What am I going to do with you?" he asked her. He flashed her a dopey grin, but she said nothing. She was still unconscious. He brushed her cheek with a finger. "I need to get you out of the rain, little one."

Where should he go? Gabe's cabin was close, but if Gabe had been the one to do this to her, then that wasn't a safe place. They couldn't stay long in the woods. There were plenty of dangers left out in the wild.

Chatwick was the obvious answer, but there was no way he'd be able to carry Sariah all the way there before the rain started up again. Not even a superhuman could do that.

There was only one answer - teleportation. Harvey had seen Gabe do it a handful of times, so he knew it was possible, and there were only the two of them.

Harvey clenched his teeth to steel his nerves and took a deep breath. He could do this. No, he had to do this. Sariah's life depended on it.

"Well, here goes nothing," he said to no one in particular.

He gave a last look at Bear. "Head to Chatwick, Bear," he told the dog. "I'm taking Sariah there, so she'll be safe."

The dog seemed to nod his head.

Harvey took another deep breath and held Sariah even tighter. In his mind's eye, he envisioned a clearing about a third of the way to Chatwick. Starting off with a smaller distance would be a good choice, he decided.

Harvey took one last look at Sariah. For her sake, he'd be successful. He was sure of it. Then he readied the spell.

Gabriel sighed. The act felt hollow somehow, like it was forced.

He took a look around at the room he was sitting in. He had a good memory for places and recognized it, which should be impossible.

Gabe was in one of the rooms in the Dusk Raven stronghold. It was one of the dozens of similar rooms in the underground maze that made up the complex. There were hundreds of tunnels and passageways that led in circuitous routes meant to confuse both friend and foe alike.

A few people, mostly the Master's servants, had maps of the complex they were forced to memorize and then burn. Gabe wasn't one of them. He just saw things and remembered them. He still let the Master's servants guide him around though, as he didn't want to make his advantage known just yet.

This room was the same one he'd been in the last time he'd come to see the Master. Back when things were going well in his life. Unlike now. He sighed again as he thought of his last meeting with the Master. He'd been so certain of his path forward at the time.

How had things taken such a turn for the worst, he wondered for the hundredth time. Try as he might, he couldn't come to grips with the way things had gone down.

Why did she turn on me? he asked himself.

He was thinking of Sariah. He hated how he'd left her in the mud. When he'd come back to check on her, that kid Harvey had been there. It hadn't been the right time to act. He'd go back for her later.

After he did something about Valerie, of course.

His lips curled into a frown, and he clenched one fist so tight that his nails dug into the skin of his palm and drew blood. That stupid dressmaker. How he hated her.

The moment he was done here, he was going back to Stratton and kill her. It wouldn't fix anything, but it would make him feel a whole hell of a lot better.

As he let his thoughts linger on the kind of torture he would inflict on her for her part in this whole thing, he started to smile again.

She'd rue the day she ever crossed him. He'd make sure of it.

Gabe didn't have long to daydream, though. A moment later, he heard a creaking noise from the wooden door as it swung inward on its hinges.

"Good afternoon," a voice called. It was the Master's. He had come for Gabriel at last.

"How is my favorite apprentice this afternoon?" the Master continued. His tone was melodic, almost like he was singing. The Master was obviously in a good mood today.

Gabe's attitude soured a little further. He groaned a bit and rolled his eyes, making sure the Master couldn't see it. He was pretty sure the man said that to everyone he taught. It wouldn't be like him to play favorites, but it would be entirely within his character to make people think he did.

The Master liked to toy with people like that. It was one of the traits Gabe admired. That and his absolute lust for power, which was what had led Gabe to seek him out originally, all those years ago.

He sighed again at the memory. Those times felt like another life now, distant and unrecognizable to the man that was sitting here in this room today.

The Master seemed to pick up on his sour mood. He came into the room slowly and shut the door softly, then walked over to him with a hint of worry on his face.

"Is something wrong with my favorite student?" the Master asked him.

Gabe scoffed. It had sounded like the Master's worry was sincere. But he knew better. The Master didn't let others' emotions affect him. Another admirable quality.

"I assure you I am quite well," Gabe answered after a moment's pause.

He must not reveal too much.

He let his features grow slack for a brief second, then straightened them again. He knew all the games to play.

Not to show fear or sadness. Not to speak unless spoken to. How to look and act. It was a long list, and normally he was fine with all of it, but today, in particular, he was finding it exhausting keeping up appearances like this.

The corners of the Master's lips turned upwards, and his eyes brightened in the dim light of the room. "Excellent," he said. "I was hoping you would say that."

Gabe spared a glance at the Master's appearance. The man had a habit of taking on new disguises all the time to keep people thrown off.

Today he was wearing a garish outfit of different-colored fabrics that shimmered in the low light. There were hints of blue and accents of green and purple. A feathered cap adorned his head. His face had a weathered look to it like he'd spent too long in the sun, and it had taken its toll. All in all, it was a confusing appearance. It seemed to exude levity and brightness, but the Master wasn't known for either of those traits.

Gabe shook his head slightly to avoid an involuntary chuckle. He wasn't sure why the man had chosen that particular look today, but he knew there would be a reason for it. The Master's odd habits always had a reason, but he wasn't here for games, he was here for power.

It was a business relationship and one that should prove profitable soon enough. And then? Well, it wouldn't do thinking about such things in the Master's presence. That could prove dangerous.

"Let's skip the pleasantries," Gabe said, breaking form. It was risky, but his patience for the Master's games was thin today.

The Master seemed slightly taken aback, but he nodded in reply. "As you wish, dearie," he said slowly.

Gabe flashed the man a quick smile. His gambit had proved successful. "I do wish it."

The Master made his way over to a chair in the room, then sat down and faced him. "I am sensing that your mood is a little off today, my child."

Gabe let out a slight laugh. "You could say that."

The Master tilted his head to the side. "Then, I am thoroughly confused."

Gabe reared his head back and furrowed his brow. Now it was his turn to be confused. The Master had dropped his decorum, and Gabe had not been expecting those words. "How so?"

"Because I brought you here today to congratulate you, but you do not seem to be in the mood to accept it." The Master glanced at one of his hands like he was inspecting it for dirt and tsked. "It's enough to make me curious, that's for sure."

"Congratulate me?" Gabe fired back. He narrowed his gaze and leveled it at the Master. "For what, exactly?"

The Master straightened and leaned forward in his chair. "For the successful completion of your grand plan, of course."

Gabe tilted his head to the side. "My grand plan?"

"To eliminate your competition and raise my esteem of you." The Master returned his gaze and smiled a little. "I must say, you succeeded far beyond my imagination."

Gabe thought fast. He hadn't really planned for everything to go down the way it had, but if the Master thought he had done it on purpose... He smiled and gave the

Master a smug look. "I didn't think you would have noticed."

The Master let out a long, hearty laugh. "Me? Not notice something as dastardly as all that? Why, how could I not?"

"His excellency is too kind," Gabe replied with a flash of a grin.

"It was remarkable how you used the girl for bait to draw out your competition and make them vulnerable. Even better how you got her to kill them, leaving your hands mostly clean in the process."

Gabe chuckled. "It wouldn't have been proper to have moved against Lucien and Severin directly, now would it?"

The Master smiled. "No, of course not. But, how did you know I would send Severin to go after Chatwick?"

"I didn't," Gabe admitted with a shrug. He let out a slight chuckle. "Honestly, I thought you were going to kill him for me after he failed to best me outside Stratton."

In his mind's eye, he went back. Sariah had just started her path of apprenticeship. He'd finally gotten her to agree to use magic to save her little friend Harvey from some Dusk Raven bandits.

Of course, no one had known at the time that he'd set the whole thing up. A few well-dropped hints in the right place was all it had taken to notify the local bandit leader there was a lone traveler who needed to part with his savings. They were all too eager to act on the intel. From there, everything had worked like clockwork. Harvey got nabbed, and Sariah had her reason to walk down his road with him for a time.

A slight twinge formed in his chest. Was that regret?

Did he feel bad about setting up Harvey to help force Sariah to learn magic? It had all worked out, hadn't it? He didn't have anything to feel bad about, anyway.

He sighed. If only things had continued, but no. Some stupid dress girl had gone and made a mess of things.

"So that was you, too?" the Master asked. He had a slightly amused look on his face. "I wasn't aware."

Gabe's attention snapped back. He nodded. "Yeah, that was me. It was one of my better ops, I must say."

"Mm, indeed." The Master rubbed his chin thoughtfully. "To tell the truth, I'd considered killing Severin on the spot for that blunder. Some stupid girl besting his whole encampment in the middle of the night? He deserved to hang just for having such lax security."

The Master paced the floor, looking toward the floor as he walked. "But when the description of that girl matched the one Lucien had failed to kill twice in Chatwick, well," he shrugged. "That was when I began to realize there was more going on."

Gabe guffawed. "Yeah, you got that right." He let a little bit of his earlier smile creep back onto his face. "A whole lot more. But enough about the past. Why did you really bring me here today?"

The Master walked over to him and placed one of his hands on Gabe's shoulder in a paternal fashion. He bowed his head. "You could have told me about her, you know," he said in a voice barely above a whisper.

Gabe's eyes went wide, and he reared back involuntarily. The Master's suggestion took him by surprise. "You mean Sariah?" he stammered.

The Master nodded once. "You could have brought her

to me. I would have been gentle." This was said with a wry smile.

Gabe felt his heart beat faster in his chest at the thought of Sariah ever meeting the Master. That was a thought that brought him no joy. He could only imagine the things the Master would want to do to her, and none of them were any good.

He shuddered and felt a small chill run down his spine as a series of unpleasant images ran across his thoughts. No, Sariah must never meet the Master. Even now, he couldn't wish that fate for her.

The Master backed up a few steps and looked Gabe in the eyes. He shrugged again. "I was only thinking of her safety, of course. It would have saved us all the trouble of the unpleasantness that followed."

"Unpleasantness?" Gabe cocked his head to the side. The word had caught him off guard.

"Mm, yes," the Master continued with a nod. "Of killing her, of course. Naturally, when she refused to continue the training, you had to kill her."

The Master's eyes were practically boring into Gabe's skull. His mind raced. For the briefest second, he thought about the last moment he'd spent with Sariah and about how he'd felt.

In his heart, he could see the truth spelled out in big letters. He knew he couldn't have killed her. Not like that. She deserved better than a pointless death.

Gabe swallowed hard and calmed his thoughts, trying to keep his head as blank as possible. "Of course," he said with a slight grimace. It was dangerous to lie to the Master, but it would have been far more dangerous to have revealed the truth. To reveal a weakness. He hoped it would pay off.

The Master continued to look at him for another moment as if daring him to flinch, but Gabe stayed put.

Did he read my thoughts? Does he know? The Master could read minds. Heck, anyone with a half-decent talent for mental magic could. And the Master was far more than decent at it.

Gabe had defenses in place just for that sort of situation. He'd long ago learned to wall off his thoughts, especially in the presence of the Master. But sitting here like this, with the Master's attention focused solely on him, bearing down on him like this, he started to doubt himself. The tiniest crack in his confidence started to form.

Then all at once, the Master shrugged and turned away. "Truly an unfortunate circumstance, I'm afraid," came his reply.

Gabe wanted to breathe a sigh of relief but knew he couldn't be so brash. No, any hope of relaxing must wait until he was alone again. So he continued to sit, his shoulders tense, and hoped the Master wouldn't notice the slight change in his posture.

After a moment of silence, he decided to try and change the subject. "Seriously, old man, why did you really bring me here today? And don't tell me it was to talk about the girl," Gabe insisted.

The Master turned on his heels and faced him once more. There was a look of glee in the man's eyes that was unlike anything Gabe had ever seen before. Was this what the Master looked like when he was happy? It was hard to know for sure, so foreign was the emotion in the man.

"Ah, yes," the Master started. He clapped his hands together. "I've good news for you."

Gabe's ears perked up. *Dare I even hope?* he thought.

His mouth suddenly felt dry, and he licked his cracked lips to try and alleviate it. "Oh?" he said at last. "You mean you?"

The Master put a hand in front of him and nodded slightly. "Yes. Well, almost, at least."

Gabe's heart sank, his momentary excitement dashed. "Oh," he said in a sullen tone.

The Master walked over and clapped him on the back. "Don't worry, lad. It will happen soon. I'm sure of it. I'm nearing a breakthrough in my magical research. Should be any day now."

Gabe let the Master keep talking, but he didn't really hear it. He'd heard the same speech from the Master many times now. He was always so positive about the results, but nothing ever seemed to come of any of the magical experiments. At least not yet.

Was it hopeless? he wondered. *Were there no magic powers left to discover? Had the limits truly been met?*

A strange thought came to him then. He didn't really know much of anything about the Master's experiments. He didn't know how they were conducted, only that the Master had promised untold power once his research was complete. And if there was one thing the Master knew well, it was how to amass power.

". . . and I promise, boy, you will be the first to hear about it when the breakthrough happens," the Master was saying at the same time that Gabe turned his attention back to the conversation.

He gave the Master a weak smile and waved dismissively with one hand. "If you say so, Ala-" He clapped his hand over his mouth to keep from saying anything further.

Had the Master been looking and caught the unintentional slip of the tongue? Gabe couldn't be certain. He was breathing still, so he assumed the answer must be a no.

Gabe let out a sigh of relief if only just a slight one. He'd almost uttered the Master's name. No one uttered the Master's true name and lived. He wasn't even supposed to know it himself, but he'd overheard it one day several years ago in a training session and couldn't very well unlearn it, could he?

Of all the Master's rules, that one was the most strictly enforced. The Master required complete secrecy at all times, especially of his identity. Somehow, Gabe knew even he, the Master's favored student, wouldn't be safe if he broke that rule. Thankfully, he'd stopped himself quickly enough.

"So what do you have planned next?" the Master asked. There was a hint of curiosity in his eyes.

Gabe gave him a wry smile. With his mental shield intact, the Master had no way to know what his intentions were. He pondered what that was like for the other man to always know what people were thinking and plotting, but not Gabe.

It was a secret weapon, and he could use any edge he could get.

Gabe shrugged. "Oh, you know, maybe do some traveling. See the sights. That sort of thing."

The Master gave a knowing smile and nodded. "Naturally. Just travel light. I'd prefer not to have any more...hiccups for a while."

With that, the Master patted him once more on the shoulder, turned and left the room.

Gabe waited several minutes to make sure he was well and truly alone. Then, he used his magic to sense the area for unsuspecting watchers and found none. He flexed his shoulder muscles and let out a huge sigh to relieve the tension.

Something had definitely been off with the Master today, and it had taken all of Gabe's wit to stay on top of the conversation the way he had. There had been several ways that scene could have ended poorly for him, and he was very glad none of them had come to fruition.

He pondered what the Master had said to him, trying to uncover any hidden truths or grains of knowledge. The Master had chosen his words carefully, but there was usually a gem hidden somewhere for Gabe to uncover.

Today, he couldn't think of any. His mind drew a complete blank.

Was I too distracted? he wondered. Probably. He knew the source of the distraction.

His thoughts turned once more to Sariah. She had been such a promising apprentice, but if he was honest with himself, she'd been more than that, too. The girl had seen something in him that no one else ever had. It hadn't been fake or manufactured like most people or a forced reaction like so many of his peers in the Dusk Ravens, but something real.

Had he thrown it all away by lying to her? Even if the

deception had been necessary, he wondered if it was too late.

He shook his head and let out a deep sigh of regret. There was no use over-thinking it now. It wouldn't do him any good or bring her back to his side.

She was gone to him. She'd made that much clear outside his hut. She wanted nothing to do with him anymore, and he couldn't blame her one bit after the way he'd treated her.

A strange feeling washed over him then, the feeling of guilt. It felt like a dagger stabbing him straight in the heart, and his whole body shook. A single tear fell from his left eye and splashed harmlessly on the ground.

He had thrown it all away, Sariah's apprenticeship, their relationship, all of it and for what? Some promise of power that might never materialize?

Gabe took in a deep breath and held it for a moment to calm his nerves.

I mustn't be so hard on myself, he told himself. He couldn't have known it was going to turn out this way. Besides, the Master always came through on his promises.

The thought made him feel a little better. He cracked his neck once and stood up. This wasn't the end. He would find Sariah, and things would go differently when he did. She'd been too emotional in the woods, but she'd see the light. He was sure of it.

First, he had an errand to take care of. He had a dress merchant to hunt down. Valerie. The mere thought of her name made his blood boil.

Gabe's teeth clenched, and he dug his nails into his

palms as a fresh wave of anger washed over him. It was exhilarating.

Out of the corner of his eye, he caught the slightest hint of movement. Gabe's whole body tensed. He looked in the direction of the movement, and his form relaxed again. It was the guide from earlier. He was back to take Gabe to the entrance of the complex.

Gabe's expression soured. Had the servant seen him crying? He shook his head and let out another sigh. It wouldn't do to have someone spinning tales about his sign of weakness around the Dusk Raven stronghold.

There was only one thing to do about it. Gabe's lips curled into a snarl. The poor kid wouldn't even see it coming.

CHAPTER TWO

Sariah groaned and stirred underneath the blankets. She tried to move her arms, and they felt unusually heavy for no reason she could discern. She tried to lift them, but they hardly budged.

The blanket was too tight, and it was constricting her.

No matter, she thought. I can always kick it loose.

A moment later, it struck her that when she'd fallen unconscious, she hadn't been under any blankets. The memories of the battle and the aftermath came rushing back, and she was left wondering both where she was and how she'd gotten there.

Laying there with her eyes closed, she couldn't be certain if she was somewhere friendly or foreign, and she had no idea who was with her or what they intended. A chill ran down her spine.

Did Gabe trap me here? Had he come back to punish me?

She supposed it was possible, but he didn't seem like

the type. His exit had been pretty final, and if he'd wanted to punish her more, why would he put her in a rather comfortable bed?

It was only at that moment that she realized she was even in a bed. Despite the precariousness of her current situation, it was pretty darn comfortable. Certainly better than the cold forest ground she'd been accustomed to sleeping on in the recent past. It wasn't as nice as the beds back at The Dragonfly in Stratton, perhaps, but still decent.

Well, then I must not be back in Stratton, either. Damn.

She groaned and bit her lip. So much for hoping the past week had been nothing but a dream. It wasn't like her to be that lucky.

If she wasn't back in Stratton, and Gabe didn't have her, then who did? And where was she? There had been no one else out in the woods with them. Sariah supposed there was no use worrying about it. If she wanted to know what was going on, she was going to have to find out the hard way.

Hesitantly, she pried one of her eyes open just a tiny bit to take in her surroundings. The room she was in was dimly lit. She could make out bits of the ceiling from where she was, but not much else.

The ceiling was wooden and looked cracked and rough as if it was in desperate need of repair. It probably was. Not a lot of buildings were built to last a lifetime these days. People just didn't have the time or the money to do stuff like that.

The ceiling wasn't a lot to go on. She'd have to be more adventurous, even if it meant letting her captor know she was awake. She was positive it was a captor and not a friend or some innocent bystander.

She opened both eyes fully and started to look around the room. The place was pretty barren. The only furniture in the room consisted of the bed she was laying in and an old rocking chair. It looked like it might burst into pieces if anyone actually tried to use it. There was a door a few feet away hanging by only one hinge, and the floor was covered in dust. There were signs of footprints leading both to and from her bed.

Oddly enough, the place felt familiar. She should know it somehow, but from where, she couldn't quite place. She was sure it would come to her. Thankfully, she appeared to be alone, at least for now, which meant she had a little time to think and act.

Where has Bear gotten off to? she wondered. The mangy mutt had stayed by her side all this time. Why wasn't he here now?

Sariah pushed those thoughts to the side and shook her head, which made her swoon a little.

She needed to escape this place first, then she could find Bear.

She started by fidgeting underneath the blanket until it was looser, then used her feet to kick at it until it came free from the bed. She let out a deep breath and got in a good stretch at the same time, finally able to move. It was still harder than it should have been, but at least it was possible now.

Instinctively, she reached for her abdomen. To her relief, her wound seemed to be gone, and her skin felt new and fresh, where it had once been painful and bloody.

Whoever her captor was, they obviously wanted her in good health. She was grateful for that.

She was also quite pleased to note she was fully dressed, though in different clothes that felt altogether too big for her. Still, it was better than thinking about some creepy guy seeing her naked.

An involuntary shiver ran up her spine at the thought, and she wrinkled her nose in disgust. That was the last thing she needed right now.

Feeling a little better about her situation, she decided to try and sit up. She did so faster than she should have, and all of the blood rushed out of her head, making her feel dizzy.

Sariah put a hand on her head and laid back down. She'd obviously been out of it for a little while. She'd have to figure out how much time had passed.

She didn't have long to think about it because a moment later, she heard the sound of footsteps outside her door. The scraping noise was loud like it was coming from someone with big, heavy feet.

Obviously, whoever it was wasn't concerned with stealth. Somehow that put her more on edge.

Her eyes searched the room for anything she could use as a weapon. Next to the bed was a withered branch that looked like an old walking stick. It was crude but better than nothing. She reached down and grabbed it, then spirited it away under the blanket to keep it out of view.

As the noise finally came to a stop outside her door, she tightened her grip on the walking stick. She'd only get one chance. If the person on the other side of the door meant her harm, she would need to act fast.

The door handle turned, and the door creaked open loudly. She swallowed a lump in her throat and braced herself.

In walked a large man, his face half-shielded in the dim light. She shot up and let loose a battle cry to startle the man, then waved the walking stick frantically in his direction.

"Sariah, please! It's me!" Harvey cried.

She squeaked and fell back onto the bed, letting the stick hit the floor. Blinking a few times, she squinted at the big man now cowering in the door frame.

Could it really be Harvey?

The big man's face finally came into focus. At the same time, Sariah's frame loosened, and all of her fears drained away. She ran over to him.

"Harvey!" she squealed. "It is you!"

She felt his strong arms encircle her, and she threw her arms around his neck, allowing herself to enjoy the warmth of the embrace for a few moments in complete silence. It felt better than it had any right to. Tears began to stream down her face, and she started to sob as she buried her face into his shoulder to make it stop.

"There, there," Harvey said. He maneuvered one of his hands to her head and stroked her hair gently for a few minutes, continuing to hold her tightly.

For those few brief minutes, Sariah felt safe and secure in a way that she hadn't since the fateful night when her parents had been killed. She needed the feeling of safety now more than she needed anything else in the world. She felt eternally grateful to Harvey for supplying it, if only for a moment.

After another minute or so of holding him, Sariah finally let go and pulled back. She sniffled once more, then rubbed her cheeks to rid them of the tears. Looking into Harvey's eyes, she saw the same warmth that she'd felt reflected there.

"Thank you," she said as soon as she could speak. She placed a hand gently on his chin and cupped it. "Thank you for always being there when I need you."

Harvey flashed her a dopey grin, breaking the spell in the process. "Aww," he let out. "You know you can always count on me. But you should really still be in bed. You need your rest after all you've been through."

He stood and beckoned for her to return to the bed.

Sariah frowned at him but complied. She was still injured, and even that small act of hers was tiring. She lay down on the bed with a big thud and turned to look at him.

Harvey moved over to the chair and started to sit down. Sariah let out a gasp and motioned to stop him, but he waved her off and sat anyway. The chair let out a loud creak but remarkably stayed in one piece.

She let out a sigh of relief. "So, how did you? How did I? I mean...where are we?"

He burst out laughing. "At my home, of course."

"But how? And Bear?"

Harvey shook his head. "It's a bit of a long story." He started by telling her how he'd woken up to find her missing in Stratton after she'd run off with Bear. He ended by describing how he'd used magic to teleport the two of them safely to Chatwick's borders and deposited her in his bedroom, sparing no detail in between.

Sariah winced every time he mentioned Gabe's name and smiled and blushed a little at the thought of being inside Harvey's bedroom. She'd thought the place looked familiar. Now she knew why.

"Sounds like quite the adventure," Sariah offered.

"Heh. You could say that again."

She opened her mouth to explain to Harvey what had happened with Gabe, and why everything had gone down the way it had, but she couldn't find the words.

"It's okay," Harvey said at last. "You don't need to explain. He obviously wasn't as great as we all made him out to be."

Sariah smiled at Harvey and gave him a nod. "You're right," she replied, but inwardly, her heart still hurt. She silently wondered if it always would.

Harvey clapped himself on the thigh. "But enough about the past! You need food to recover!" He got up and started heading for the door.

Sariah's stomach gurgled at the mention of food. She smiled up at Harvey. "You always did know how to treat a lady!" she called after his fleeing form.

She laid back down in bed and tried to close her eyes and wait patiently for Harvey to bring her food, but her stomach wouldn't let her. She warred with her stomach for a moment longer, but in the end, she got up carefully and went down the stairs after him.

Harvey smiled a contented smile. He'd spent the previous night sharing a hearty meal of lamb stew with Sariah, and now she was back upstairs in his room, presumably resting. For the first time in weeks, things finally felt like they were falling into place.

This was the kind of life he'd always dreamed of having with her. Of course, not until they were both older. In his earlier dreams, her parents had still been very much alive, and none of this Gabe and Stratton business had ever happened, either. Things never worked out in real life quite like they did in dreams, though.

But last night hadn't been a dream. It had been real. Sariah had been there, happy to see him and spend time with him, despite all of the recent darkness. She'd even spilled some of the details of what had happened. That had been plenty good enough for him.

Now it was morning, and he was going to check on her. He started up the stairs, carrying a platter full of eggs and oatmeal, her favorite breakfast. Nothing less would do for today.

A smile played across his face, and he hummed a silly tune from his childhood as he walked. He could just tell that somehow, today was going to be a good day.

Harvey knocked on the door to his bedroom gently. He heard a small groan from the other side and some shuffling.

"Come in," Sariah's voice beckoned. He obliged.

"I've brought breakfast," he announced as he walked through.

Sariah took an appreciative whiff, and her lips curled into a broad smile. "Eggs and oatmeal? You remembered!" Her eyes were bright.

Harvey set the platter down on the side of her bed and

nodded. "Of course, I did. How could I forget all those times you went around stealing eggs from Mrs. Hensworth's house as a kid to make it?"

Her face turned a bright shade of red, and she buried her face in the blanket. "Whoops," she offered. Her voice was partly muffled by the quilt.

"Oh, don't worry, I'm pretty sure she was on to you anyway and just didn't care."

She peeked over the covers cautiously. "You think?"

He nodded again. "I do." He speared one of the eggs with a fork and swallowed it in one bite. He was feeling pretty hungry too.

She gave him a demure smile and followed suit. The two ate in silence for several minutes, sharing furtive glances all the while.

At last, he spoke. "So, what would you like to do today?"

Sariah shrugged. "Probably rest some more. I'm still pretty tired from everything."

Harvey flashed her a dopey grin. "Makes sense."

"Then, I guess I don't know. I'll have to start tracking him down. Gabriel, I mean."

His expression soured, and not just because of the mention of Gabe's name. He gave her a stern look. "Come now, you can't mean that, can you? He practically killed you last time!"

She nodded. "I know. I was there, remember?" Her eyes narrowed. "You weren't."

Heat rose to his cheeks, and his eyes darkened. "That wasn't my fault!" he shot back.

Sariah put out a hand in a defensive position. "I'm

sorry. That was uncalled for." She lowered her head. "I shouldn't have said that."

Harvey wanted to growl, but he suppressed the desire. It wouldn't do him any good. He brushed his clothing to calm himself. "No, I'm sorry. The last weeks have been really trying for you. I can only imagine how hard it was."

She motioned for him to sit down next to her on the bed. He complied, and she put her head on his shoulder. He placed an arm around her, and they sat there for a moment in silence. For a moment, he thought she was going to cry again, but nothing happened.

When she finally spoke, her voice was surprisingly firm and calm. "I have to find him, Harvey, and put a stop to him. I have to put a stop to all of them."

Sariah was referring to the Dusk Ravens. The revelation that Gabe was still one of them had come as somewhat of a shock to Harvey, but it had passed quickly. Everything made much more sense with that bit of information.

"You don't mean you're still going to go after them, do you?" He furrowed his brow. "After all you've been through, you still want to go through with it?"

She hesitated for a moment. "Of course, I am. I cannot rest until they're all gone."

Harvey got up off the bed. He huffed in disgust. "You can't possibly mean that."

She put her hands on her hips and glared at him. "How could I mean anything else?"

He turned his head to face her but left the rest of his body facing away. "Come on, Sariah! These are dangerous people. You're no match for them out there all by yourself!"

Sariah turned her head to hide her expression. "Who says I'd be alone? Or are you abandoning me, too?"

Harvey let out a slight yelp. He turned around fully and placed a hand on her shoulder. "I didn't mean it like that. Of course, I'm still there for you. To the ends of the Irth, right? It's just…"

"It's just what?" she demanded, still not willing to face him. "That I'm a girl? That I'm not skilled enough? Or just that you don't have any faith in me?"

The words cut like a knife, stabbing straight at his heart. He felt a tightening in his chest. "Come on, Sariah. You know that's not how I think. I just don't understand how you could possibly still want to go after them. How can you hope to defeat them without our best ally?"

She turned to face him fully, then. There was a look of fierce determination in her eyes and a scowl on her face. "Do you really think they'll leave me alone after all I've done? Do you think I have a choice?"

Harvey shrugged. "Maybe."

Sariah growled and turned back around.

He pulled on her shoulder to try and turn her to face him, but she wouldn't budge. "Look, they've got dozens of men. Hundreds, probably. Sure, you killed a few of them, but if you give up now and stay here with me, who's to say they won't be content with that?"

He heard her groan and her shoulders slacked. "You still don't get it, do you?"

"Get what, exactly?"

"They killed my parents." She turned. This time, there was a sadness in her eyes that hadn't been there before, as well as a hint of fire. "I can't simply forgive that. I caught a glimpse of their leader's true intentions when I fought Lucien, and I can't allow that to come to pass. Someone has to stop them, and if no one else is willing, it has to be me."

Harvey started pacing around the room. "So what's your grand plan?" he demanded, his tone angry. "Run up and throw sticks at them?"

Sariah rolled her eyes and growled. "Oh, come on! Of course not! Valerie told me about some people who could help. People who think like me. I'm sure they'd be willing to help."

"A group of people you've never seen or heard of until last week is magically going to help you, are they?" he scoffed.

Sariah looked sheepish. She shrugged. "Maybe." She shot him an icy glare. "It's better than no plan, at least!"

Harvey threw up his hands in defeat. "Fine. Have it your way." He paced around the room a few times, muttering under his breath about stubborn women and how hard it was to be him.

She got up and placed a hand gently on his forearm. The feel of her cool skin against his gave him pause. He looked at her, and her eyes seemed intensely sad.

"You're not giving up on me, too, are you?" She sniffed a little as she spoke.

"Of course not, Sariah," he told her, his mouth agape. A huge sigh escaped his lips. "I'd never abandon you."

Her features softened, and her eyes brightened. "I'm so happy to hear you say that." She squeezed his hand, and he pressed back. Standing there looking at her at that moment, he felt complete.

"We'll leave tomorrow after breakfast, then," she said with a grin.

Harvey rolled his eyes. The moment had passed, and he could feel anger welling up again. "Sariah, you could have died out there! Almost did, in fact. You can't be racing off again so soon."

"Well, it's not like I have much left to live for!" she snapped, turning her head and looking at the wall.

"Agh!" he wailed. He pulled on his face and started pacing again. "Is that what you think? What about Chatwick? What about all your friends here?"

What about me? he added silently. Inside, his heart was breaking.

Sariah glared at him. "Just like you to pull the friend card, huh? Just how do you think our 'friends' are going to feel the next time the Master decides to invade, huh?"

He opened his mouth to say something, but nothing came. Instead, he wagged a finger at her and turned away, his cheeks burning.

"Look," he said slowly. "When I saw you out there in the mud, on the brink of death...I don't know how to describe it. I don't think I could take it if I found you like that again."

He took in a deep breath to try and calm his nerves, but it was mostly ineffective. After a moment, he felt her hand on his back, moving up and down gently.

"I'm sorry," Sariah told him. He turned to look at her, and she flashed him a slight grin. "I know this has been hard on you, too."

Harvey grabbed her hand in his. "Thank you, Sariah."

"It's just, I can't rest as long as the Dusk Ravens are out there, and—"

"Ugh!" He spat in disgust, throwing his hands up. "Look, let's just talk about it tomorrow, okay?"

Sariah stared at him wild-eyed and barely nodded.

He pulled on his face again. "I have to go into town to get some more food and supplies. Now that you're awake, you're going to need to restore your energy."

With one last look at her empty eyes, he turned and opened the door. A furry form lunged through the opening and swept past Harvey's legs, barking like mad all the while.

"Bear!" Sariah exclaimed.

Harvey walked into the hallway and slammed the door, then took another deep breath. That had not gone well at all. He shook his head and went downstairs.

She'll see the light in the morning, he reasoned. *She has to.*

Sariah woke up with a start. It was well after dark, and she was still in Harvey's room. He was nowhere to be seen, presumably in the main room downstairs. Bear was at her feet, breathing contentedly.

Absentmindedly, she rubbed Bear's head, and he gave an appreciative growl in response.

She stretched and let out a muffled groan. Her body still ached from the fight with Gabe. Inwardly, she wondered what she was doing, awake at this odd hour.

She got up, and gave her legs a good stretch one at a time, then stretched her whole body. It groaned in response, and her knees practically buckled, so she quickly got back into bed. It seemed like her body wasn't quite ready to be on the road again just yet. A little more sleep, and she was sure she'd be fine.

A loud snoring noise from outside her door startled her. She walked over and peered underneath the crack. She smiled. Harvey was there, fast asleep and snoring away.

The poor man was probably worried she'd run off on him again. Sariah supposed she deserved that. She'd done it often enough. Here she was, awake at almost midnight, thinking about doing that very thing yet again.

She let out a heavy sigh.

As much as she desperately wanted to believe Harvey would be there for her no matter what on this quest, she knew better. The way he'd talked at her, all angry, was unlike him.

He'd made one thing clear. He didn't approve of her running after Gabe and the Master. Not anymore.

Her hands balled into fists involuntarily as the thought incensed her. How could he be content running away? How can he just let it all go? That wasn't fair. Harvey had earned the right to live as he chose. He'd already done and given up so much for her. He deserved to live a simple life if that's what he wanted.

It's just not the life for me…

Still, she couldn't walk out on him again, could she? The poor fool would just run after her, and then what? He could end up dead, or worse - captured and tortured again. A shudder ran down her spine as she remembered the first time he'd been caught. She couldn't handle being the cause of that happening again.

No, she had to protect him. But how? She rubbed her

chin. It seemed she couldn't leave him, but she couldn't make him go with her, either.

Exhaustion crept into her thoughts. She was still tired. She supposed she could worry about it later.

Sariah rubbed her eyes and headed back over to the bed. She punched the pillow once to take the edge off her mood, then laid down and stared up at the ceiling, wishing she was anywhere but where she was.

CHAPTER THREE

Harvey let out a slow moan and turned over. The sun was peeking into his house, streaming through the window in the hallway and dancing on his face, willing him to wake up.

Something hard was sticking into his side. He moved his hand and felt around. It was the hilt of a dagger. He must have gone to sleep armed.

It seemed odd, but he supposed it must be a habit now after months of marching, training, and combat. He moved the hilt into a better spot and turned over fully onto his side, away from the sun so he could steal a few extra moments of sleep before he'd have to get up and face the day.

What a day it was going to be. Sometime during the middle of the night, he'd come to a decision. He'd go with her. He'd follow her on her quest until the ends of Irth if he needed to. Somehow, deep down, he'd known that even during the fight. He couldn't abandon his best friend.

So today, he would set out on another journey with her,

to find these strange friends Sariah mentioned that would help her out, he supposed, and whatever else besides. That is if these people were even real.

All Sariah had was the name of a town and a vague direction.

Maybe the townsfolk would have some clues. They had been occupied by Dusk Raven soldiers for several days, not that long ago. Someone might have overheard something useful.

He'd hit up several of his usual suspects yesterday while gathering supplies. Jackson, the town priest, Tim, the guardsman, and a few others, but no one had had much to offer. He'd have to cast a wider net.

The young man opened his eyes and realized he was staring at his bedroom doorway. He'd kept guard outside Sariah's door for a little while last night and must have fallen asleep.

Am I really that worried she'd run away on me? he thought. After yesterday's conversation, he had been. So, he'd placed himself outside her door.

That wasn't fair to her. She deserved the benefit of the doubt, now more than ever.

He stretched and smiled. It hadn't budged at all last night, and he would have heard it if it had. The door was old and in desperate need of grease. It made a terrible creaking noise every time it moved.

Sariah and Bear were still in there, both probably still sound asleep. It was early yet.

Harvey decided to leave them to it and go make some breakfast. He scurried down the stairs and whipped up more eggs and oatmeal. He was a much better chef than

Sariah, so he'd rather he was the one who did the cooking anyway.

As he set about the task, thoughts of the coming journey clouded his mind. He thought about finding new friends and fighting against the Dusk Ravens yet again.

Was he certain he wanted to go after them? They'd kidnapped him, caused some damage to his hometown, and they'd killed Sariah's parents. Those facts alone were enough to make him hate them.

Being home again and seeing the rather poor state of mental health his own father was in, was tugging at his brain, telling him it wouldn't be so bad to stay, either.

He wasn't sure the Dusk Ravens would come after them again. He shook his head. They'd tried a few times already and failed.

Still, there would be no persuading Sariah otherwise. He'd tried that yesterday and failed miserably. That girl could really set her mind in stone when she wanted to. It was a quality he generally admired.

He shrugged and headed back upstairs. There would be time enough to worry about it later. Sariah was still weak, and if he tried, he could probably convince her to stick around in town for another day or two.

Then he'd just have to wait and see.

Harvey knocked twice on the door but strode into the room without waiting for an answer. With a broad grin plastered on his face, he took in the scene in the room before him.

The blood drained quickly from his face, and he dropped the breakfast platter, the plates shattering as they hit the ground.

His eyes went wide as the truth of the situation came crashing down on him.

Bear was snoozing on one corner of the bed, oblivious to all of the commotion. But Sariah was another matter. Sariah was gone.

***

Padron rounded another corner on the footpath and took in a deep breath. The forest air of the Alpenwood was crisp this morning. In another few weeks or so, the days would grow shorter and the leaves would turn, heralding the start of Autumn.

He loved the Autumn time. All the bright colors of the leaves, the reds, the oranges, the browns. Those colors felt more natural to him than the bright greens, so used to living underground as he was.

Up ahead, he could make out the walls of Chatwick peeking through the trees. His journey had taken far longer than he'd expected, but he was almost home again.

It felt good to be back. The Heights had been beautiful and most welcoming, as always, but they were a part of his past. Chatwick was where he belonged now. He knew it surer than he knew anything else.

He wondered for probably the hundredth time what Harvey and Sariah were up to. Had they returned home while he'd been out? How had her quest to avenge her parents' deaths gone? He supposed he'd find out the answers soon enough.

Padron spotted a clearing up ahead and knew he was

almost home. He took the last few steps through the trees in a few strides, bouncing all the way.

When the trees cleared, he saw Chatwick. His home. The main gate looked like it had suffered some damage while he had been gone. A bad storm, perhaps, but otherwise, the town looked just like he remembered.

He took a big whiff and caught the smell of baking bread wafting over the clearing. It was still early, and Thomasson's bakery was apparently still in full swing.

His mouth watered as he thought about their bread. They made the best loaves. Sometimes he'd order two to go with his stew after a particularly long day in the mines. The memory was a sweet one, and it made his heart swoon.

Padron started running, eager to get back home.

In the back of his mind, he wondered if anyone would remember the incident in the mines he'd caused when he'd left two months ago.

He shook his head. He doubted it. There had been dozens of people in the mine that day and no witnesses. There was no way anyone could trace it back to him.

A grimace crossed his lips. He'd been in quite the hurry, then, and for a good reason. Things would be calmer now.

He was so lost in thought that he barely noticed a big young man rush past him, barreling out of the main gate at high speed. The poor fool was making a beeline for the trees behind them, running as though his life depended on it.

Padron smiled at the recklessness of youth. But something about the young man sparked his memory. He could have sworn he'd recognized the young man, even if he had grown quite a bit in just a couple of short months.

"Harvey?" he called out, turning in the same breath.

The young man running for the trees stopped cold in his tracks and turned slowly, a big dopey grin on his face. "Padron?" Harvey asked, staring at him, his eyes wide with wonder.

Padron's lips curled upward into a broad smile. "It is you, lad! Come 'ere!" He held his hands out wide.

Harvey ran forward and embraced him. The lad's grip felt tighter than it had a few months ago when he'd left with Sariah. The boy had grown.

He embraced Harvey for a moment, then pushed him backward. "Let me get a good look at ya. I feel like I havna seen ya in ages!" he exclaimed. He took in the boy's face. His chin had hardened, and there was a hint of stubble there. The boy's eyes looked sterner. There was a fierceness that hadn't been there before and also concern. There were lines underneath his eyes. The lad was clearly worried about something serious.

"I didn't think I'd see you again," Harvey said, smiling at him. "When I got back a few days ago, I asked around about you, but the rearick in town said you'd left without warning two months ago."

Padron nodded. "Aye, lad, that I did. I can't be bothered to stay away forever now, can I? Can't let ya get inta too much trouble."

Harvey bit his lip and glanced over his shoulder. He was being kind, but his true intentions were plain on his face. He was chasing after something or someone.

"Come now lad, what's worryin' ye?" Padron

demanded.

The young man let out a big sigh. "I never could fool you for long, could I?" he asked.

Padron shook his head.

Harvey's eyes darted around a few times before settling back on his face. "It's Sariah," he said in a whisper, his voice cracking. "She's gone."

The blood drained from Padron's face, and a terrible thought came to him. "She didn't?"

Harvey shook his head furiously. "No, it's nothing like that. She's alive. At least, I think she is. She wasn't in her room this morning and…"

Padron clapped him on the shoulder. Harvey seemed to almost buckle under the weight of the rearick's giant hand. He looked up at the lad. "I'm sure she'll come 'round again soon enough. We couldna separate tha two a ya fer longer than a day or two, even as youths."

Harvey's face brightened a little as the rearick spoke. He nodded. "I'm sure you're right," he admitted at last.

"Come now, let's go grab a few mugs of ale down at Talesin's old place, and we can swap tales. I've got some pretty burnin' hot information to share meself," Padron offered. "Unless Talesin done gone up in smoke while I was out, that is." He said the last bit in a playful tone.

Harvey chuckled and shook his head. "No, it's still there. My father still spends most of his day there. Heck, he's probably there now and it's barely morning."

"Come on then. Let's go have a long chat. Man to man."

The young man took another long, furtive look over his shoulder. He seemed to stare off into the distance for what felt like an eternity. A great war must be taking place in his head, Padron surmised. He wondered which side would win.

At long last, he turned to face Padron. He gave the rearick another nod. "All right." His lips formed another dopey grin. "Sounds like a plan."

Padron burst out into a hearty laugh. "That's me boy!" He clapped the boy on the back again, harder than the last time, and the boy almost went sprawling. He barely managed to keep himself upright.

Then, arms locked, the two strode forward into the town.

Harvey strode through the door of Talesin's establishment, still locking arms with Padron. It was good to have the man with him again. Something about it just felt right and made his current pain a little more bearable.

He looked around and spotted his father in a corner, nursing a mug of ale. The man spent a good portion of his days here, drowning his sorrows. He'd never been the same since his wife—Harvey's mother—had died.

Harvey still felt the loss keenly himself, but he couldn't afford to spend his life wasting away. Someone had to keep the money flowing in. He shook his head to clear it and looked over at the barkeep.

"Talesin!" he cried. "Two mugs of your finest ale for Padron and me here!" he shouted.

The barkeep grinned and nodded at him. "Harvey! So good to see you." He glanced over at the boy's father. "You're not normally here so early, son. Everything okay?"

Harvey wondered for a moment if Talesin's concern was for Harvey, or for the possibility of losing the income from one of his most faithful patrons for a day. Usually, he didn't come to collect his father until well after supper.

That was a little unfair, he decided. He shouldn't assume the worst. He shook his head and grinned back at Talesin. "Naw, just thought I'd see what all the fuss was about for myself."

"Excellent." The barkeep made a broad sweeping motion with his hands. "Sit anywhere you like. I'll have that ale brought out straight away."

Harvey looked over at Padron. "Shall we?" The rearick nodded, and they made their way to a table in the corner farthest from his father. He had no desire for his dad to hear anything the two spoke about right now. It would only cause him trouble later.

No sooner had they sat down than two mugs of frothy ale appeared at their table. Harvey looked at the barmaid and flashed her a dopey grin before she could disappear. She returned the smile then scurried off.

The young man took a whiff of the ale and wrinkled his nose. It smelled of yeast and something far worse. He'd never really had any alcoholic beverages before, as at seventeen, he was still considered too young by most.

He poked at the frothy bubbles, and they dissipated under his touch. He found that odd, but shook his head and lifted the mug to his lips anyway. The bubbles tickled his upper lip a little, and he took a big swig. He practically choked on the beverage as it slid down his throat, burning all the way and tasting of old oats.

People drank this stuff willingly? Harvey set the mug

down and pushed it away from him, then looked over at Padron. The rearick didn't seem to have the same aversion and had already downed half his ale.

The rearick let out a rather loud belch. "Amazing stuff, ain't it?" he said, pointing at Harvey's mug.

Harvey shrugged. "It's...interesting."

Padron bust out laughing and slapped himself on the thigh. "Aye, that's a word fer it. I'll admit, me lad, it ain't got nothin' on the brews they make back in my old home town. That stuff'll put hair on yer chest fer sure."

Harvey gave him a weak smile. This was the weak stuff? He didn't even want to think about how awful the more potent brews could be. He feigned taking another drink so it would look like he was enjoying himself. He didn't want to disappoint Padron.

"Sounds great," he said at last.

Padron laughed again and side-eyed him. "It's all right, lad. Yer a bit wet behind the ears yet." He reached over and ruffled Harvey's hair with one hand. "Ye'll develop a taste fer the stuff when ye get older."

Harvey gave him another grin. He sure hoped the rearick would be wrong about that one but shrugged it off. He had other things on his mind, like Sariah. He hoped she was safe, wherever she was, but he couldn't be certain.

He'd been fairly sure she wasn't going to run off on him this time, but he'd been wrong. He couldn't figure out how she made it out of the room without him knowing. That still nagged at him and made him fear for the worst.

The young man chewed on his lip as he thought about her, and then all of a sudden, his thoughts grew calmer. He could somehow sense that she was okay. As quickly as the quiet thought had come, it passed and the moment was gone. He was back to staring at his rearick companion and trying to pretend to drink a giant mug of foul-smelling ale.

He went back to mindlessly chewing on his lip and looking aimlessly about the room.

Padron noticed his behavior, and a moment later the rearick slugged him on the shoulder. It stung a little, but it brought him back to his senses.

"Ow," Harvey complained, rubbing the wound. It was going to bruise for sure. "What was that for?"

The rearick shrugged. "Just making sure yer still with me." He gave Harvey a broad smile and motioned for the barkeep to send over another mug of ale. "Now, lad, why don't ye tell me everything that's on yer mind. What happened after ye skipped town with that big good-for-nothing."

Harvey cocked his head to the side. Padron was obviously referring to Gabriel. Had the rearick known back then that the man was bad news? If so, then why hadn't he said anything? He shook his head. Such thoughts would do no good.

The young man let out a long sigh, then settled back in his chair. "This might take a while," he cautioned.

Padron nodded.

Harvey started on his tale. He told the rearick everything that had happened, sparing no detail. Around an hour later, he finally finished his story.

The rearick was staring at him with big, round eyes like he could hardly believe what he'd heard. He blinked a few times. "Magic?" the rearick said, shaking his head. "That there's bad news, even fer ye."

Harvey shrugged. "It has its uses. It saved me once, and it's saved Sariah a few times now. Like anything, it's a tool, and it's more about the wielder than what is being wielded."

Padron chuckled and clapped him on the same shoulder he'd punched earlier. "Aye, yer still a small lad, but in some ways yer wiser than I might have reckoned."

"So, how about you?" Harvey asked. "What have you been up to? Tell me your tale."

The rearick's eyes went wide, and he pointed at himself. "Me? Ah, compared to that, I ain't done hardly a thing me boy. Jus' went and examined the mines then took a little trip back home, I did. Certainly nothin' as grand as all that."

Harvey smiled. "I guess it was something. Still, you sounded a lot more convincing in the forest. What gives?"

Padron scratched his chin. "Ah. That. Well, 'twas my reason fer bein' in tha mines, in tha first place, lad. I knew somethin' screwy musta been going on down there fer there to be such increased security after you left."

Harvey's eyes went wide. "Something happened at the mines? When?"

"Calm down, lad. Everythin's fine down there. It weren't like that," Padron insisted.

Harvey breathed a sigh of relief and begged the rearick to continue.

Padron took another swig of his ale and set the empty mug down. It was his third of the morning. Harvey wondered where the man put it all.

"It's just, somethin' didn't sit quite right with me after the incident with Sariah's parents," Padron started after a moment. "I reckoned they must be hidin' somethin' down in those mines. Why else would they have targeted her like that?"

The young man bobbed his head. That did make sense.

"So, I went an' looked fer meself. An' what did I find?" The rearick's eyes narrowed and they darted around the room. He leaned in close. "Amphoralds."

He spoke the word like it should mean something, but Harvey just blinked once. "Amphoralds?" he repeated.

Padron nodded. "Aye. Terrible things, lad. They're little gems that store magic, an' power terrible weapons an' devices. If they was after the amphoralds in the mine, then tha Dusk Raven's actions start to make sense. I just wish I still had mine to show ye."

The rearick seemed lost in thought, but Harvey's mind was racing. Things were starting to click into place—the attacks on Sariah, the secrecy, the occupying the town. It hadn't been about him and Sariah at all. Well, not directly. It had been about amassing power.

If the attacks on Sariah had been nothing but a diversion, was it possible the Dusk Ravens were still here, toiling away in the mines right under their very noses? It seemed a likely answer. Which meant…

"The mines are in trouble!" both Harvey and Padron said at the same time.

Harvey ducked his head and lowered his voice. "What should we do? We have to stop them and root the corruption out of our town once and for all."

Padron nodded. "Aye, I'm with ye, lad. We must go to tha mines at once."

Harvey put out a hand to keep the rearick from getting

up. "No, we need to be strategic about this. We don't know who at the mines we can or cannot trust. We need a plan."

The rearick seemed taken aback. "We can trust me people. They wouldna side with no Dusk Ravens."

Harvey nodded. "You're probably right. Okay, that gives me an idea. We'll meet up with them tonight and get them to take us into the mines tomorrow. Once inside, we'll set the rest of my plan into action."

<hr>

Harvey shifted, trying to get comfortable. It was the morning of the next day, and he was under a blanket in a minecart. There were a few tools sticking out at odd angles to give the impression that the blanket was hiding equipment instead of a person, but said tools also had a way of digging into his back.

Padron was hiding in another minecart in front of him.

The night before they'd gone to the remaining rearick in town after supper time, and the two had explained everything. Once the other rearick had heard, they'd been only too happy to help.

Now he just had to hope the guards at the new gate stations wouldn't notice anything amiss. All he had to do was stay put and not move for a little while longer, and they would be through the gate.

Secrecy had been paramount to his plan. If the Dusk Ravens really were in charge, they would be looking for someone who fit his description to approach the mines directly. He wasn't about to give them that kind of satisfaction. Not yet, at least.

In his mind, he thought about what he'd do to them for harassing his townsfolk. The thought brought a smile to his face.

Just then, a pickaxe poked him just below the ribs. It stung and felt like it had possibly drawn a little blood, but he held back a moan of pain. They were almost at the guard stations, and he couldn't give away his position.

"Good morning, Justine," a gruff voice called out. Justine was the name of the rearick pushing his cart. "Headed to the mine early today?"

Harvey cursed under his breath. Was his plan going to be foiled by an overly chatty guard?

Justine tsked. "It's Sunday, Trevor. I always go to tha mines early on Sunday."

Harvey heard a slight chuckle from the guard.

"Oh yeah," Trevor's voice said. "I forgot. Speaking of, it's almost time for me to end my shift. Will I see you at Talesin's tonight?"

Is this guy going to talk forever? Harvey wondered. In spite of himself, he let out a slight groan.

Justine laughed. "Aye, I'll be there, lad. Now be a good boy an' let me on through," her voice commanded.

"Oh. Right." He heard the sound of feet scuffling on stone, then it stopped. "Be on your way, darlin'."

The cart started moving again. As they passed through the gate station, he heard the sound of someone getting slapped on the ass. Justine chuckled a little. "Oh, Trevor, you lech!" she shouted in a sultry tone.

Did she actually like that creep? He tried not to think about it. It was probably part of her cover.

Harvey let out a slight sigh of relief. He wanted to move

to wipe some sweat off his brow, but he knew he couldn't just yet. Just a little bit further, and they'd be through.

A few minutes later, the area around him darkened. His shoulders slackened a bit. They were in the mines at last.

Phase one complete.

The minecart came to a stop, and both Harvey and Padron got out from underneath the blankets. Harvey looked over at Justine and her friend Bailey, who had been the one to push Padron's cart.

He nodded at them. "Thank you both," he said. "You've been a tremendous help."

Justine waved at him. "Aww, it ain't nothin'," she said with a smile.

Harvey rummaged around in the minecart and pulled out his sword. It shone dully in the low light. He looked over at Padron. The rearick had his trusty battle-axe at the ready in his own palms.

"Ready to assault the mines?" he asked his friend with a broad grin on his face.

Padron grinned back at him and nodded. "Let's do this."

The two started down the mine shaft. A moment later, they heard a grating noise behind them, followed by a loud clank and the sound of metal scraping against metal.

A chill ran up Harvey's spine. Quickly, he turned and ran back toward the entrance, only to find it barred over by a massive metal door.

Panic started to set in, and Harvey swallowed hard. His plan had backfired. They had made it to the mines, all right, but they had not gone unnoticed.

They were trapped.

CHAPTER FOUR

"*Scheisse!*" Sariah swore. She looked down at her foot. There was a new, tiny hole in her shoe staring back at her. Some sort of needle had managed to stick into her boot.

Her foot was throbbing, and it felt wet like there was fresh blood on it. She swore again and sat down to look at it. Taking off the shoe as carefully as she could, she inspected her throbbing appendage. There on the side, a small needle was indeed sticking out.

Gingerly, she grabbed and pulled it. It was barbed, so a little bit of skin came with it. She bit her lip to fight against the pain and swore again for good measure. Then, she got a bit of cloth out of her pack and wrapped the new wound to stem the bleeding.

"No wonder mages just teleport everywhere," she groaned.

In fact, she'd done the same herself this very morning. At first, she'd assumed teleportation magic was beyond her abilities, but after Harvey had opened up about how he'd managed it, she figured it was worth a shot.

After fussing with how to accomplish it for nearly an hour, she'd finally managed to jump almost accidentally. Thankfully, she'd managed to head in the right direction, though it had taken her some time to get her bearings after she had arrived.

It was a stalwart reminder that teleporting without knowing for sure where one was going was a very bad idea, and she hadn't tried it again.

Plus, it had cost her the chance to take Bear along. Her thoughts drifted toward her animal companion. What would he think of her taking off without him? What would any of them think?

Was there anything on Irth she could possibly do to make up for it this time?

She let out a tired breath and closed her eyes. After this, she was quite certain Harvey would never speak to her again. Bear would probably abandon her, too. She wouldn't blame them, after how many times she had run off without them. She deserved her fate, really.

Sariah had felt it necessary, though. It was the only way she could keep Harvey safe and prevent him from getting killed on her behalf. She nodded once to reassure herself, but it didn't help.

Now that she was out in the wilderness, alone once again, and heading toward an unfamiliar and potentially hostile situation, she wasn't as sure it had been the right decision.

She shook her head and tried to calm her thoughts. The people up ahead would be friendly. Valerie had assured her of that. She had to believe in the old woman's last words to her, at the very least.

Her foot throbbed again, so she gave it another glance. She'd done a decent job of applying the bandage, and it hurt less than it had before. It also looked like the bleeding had finally stopped.

If only I was better at healing magic, she mused. Maybe someday. She took a deep breath and put her boot back on, but stayed on the ground for another few minutes. It was getting to be breakfast time, and she could use a little more sustenance.

Sariah rummaged around in her pack. There were a few days' worth of rations, mostly tasteless stuff—stuff she'd had left over in her pack from before—but it was better than starving. She pulled out a random wedge of something hard and dry and tore off a chunk with her teeth.

She chewed on it for a while, then washed it down with a swig from her canteen. Her thoughts were still on Harvey. He deserved better than what she'd done to him.

The poor guy was probably worried sick about her. She resolved to do something about it. She centered herself and focused on an image of Harvey in her mind, and uttered a few nonsense words while she did so.

It took a moment, for they were quite far apart, but eventually, she was able to feel his thoughts at the edge of hers. She sent him good thoughts about her. She tried to tell him she was safe and well and would write to him soon, but she doubted any of it actually made it through. The distance was just too great.

Still, maybe at least the well wishes would reach his mind and give him some comfort.

"Well," she said. "Might as well get to it. This Talon's Reach place isn't going to find itself."

Sariah got up and tentatively placed weight on her injured foot. It held up nicely with just a tiny shock of pain. Grimacing, she supposed it would have to do.

Maybe I'll try to heal it anyway. She spent a moment trying to summon healing magic to her, but in so doing, her thoughts went back to how Gabe had healed her in the woods outside Chatwick.

Her throat started to constrict, and she wondered for probably the hundredth time why things had worked out the way they had.

Then she shook her head and let out a deep breath. There was no use in worrying about it anymore. It wouldn't change the past or make Gabe any less her enemy, no matter how much it hurt her to think of him like that.

When the moment had passed, she was surprised to find that she'd been crying, and fresh tears were streaming down both of her cheeks. She let out a long sigh.

Will it ever get easier?

Probably, she mused. She'd heard that heartbreak symptoms got better with time. At least, that's what all the adults in her life kept telling her while she was growing up. Now it was time for her to find out for herself.

Joy, she thought wryly—just my luck.

She shoved the thoughts from her mind and got back to the task at hand. Healing would have to wait, so she'd have to make do. She took a step forward, only to be greeted by a small jolt of pain that ran up her leg from the wound on her foot. Her face contorted into a grimace, and she bit her lip.

This was not going to cut it. She'd have to do something more to help lessen the pain.

With few resources to work with, she decided to ball up some extra cloth and put it into the spot in her shoe underneath the injured area to cushion her foot a little better. Then, she got up and tried again.

Another jolt greeted her, but it was less severe. Manageable, if not by much. She shrugged. It would have to do. Supposedly this magical resistance town wasn't much further if it even existed at all.

Sariah took a few more steps, wincing with each one. They got a little easier as she went along, and the cloth settled into a good position in her shoe. By the time she'd gone a hundred paces, the pain had subsided to a dull throb that she could ignore without too much trouble.

Her eyes scanned the horizon. The area was fairly clear, with very little tree growth. There were patches here and there, but it wasn't much like the forests of the Alpenwood. Off in the distance to the east, several mountains pushed up into the sky, blocking the remainder of the horizon. Their tops were barren this time of year, but in the winter, they probably held lots of fresh snow.

All in all, it was a beautiful area, but there was no sign of this Talon's Reach that Valerie had talked about. Of course, she hadn't had time to fill her in on too many details, and even if she had, it would be hard for Sariah to know just how close she really was since she'd teleported most of the way.

That, and she'd never been there.

Her foot throbbed a little harder then, and she groaned and came to a halt to look at it. She pulled off her shoe and inspected the bandage. It looked fine. The blood hadn't soaked all the way through it.

Maybe she needed another adjustment to the padding. She played with the cloth a little and folded it into neat little sheets, then placed it back under her injury and tested it. It was a success. The pain was back to a dull throb.

With a satisfied nod, she started her march forward again. That's when she caught sight of a walled city in the distance. It looked small, but she knew how deceptive distances could be.

Ahead of her on the worn path stood an old fortress. Its stone walls jutted out of the ground at straight angles, breaking the serenity of the countryside with stark gray colors. The center tower of the fort must have been a hundred feet tall if it was twenty, and the stone walls stretched out wide in both directions.

It was enough to make her jaw drop open in amazement. She'd thought Stratton was something, and it was, but this was even more amazing to behold somehow. To think that someone would have taken the time to gather so many stones together in one place.

Crazy.

When she got closer, she started to see the cracks in the massive stone walls and a few patches where the moss was growing on them. The giant wooden door in the front was rotten in a few places, and the tower had a gaping hole in the roof that shouldn't be there.

Upon closer inspection, it looked like the fortress was in far worse condition than she'd originally surmised, though she supposed it could still do a good job of dissuading people from attacking.

A gasp of wonder escaped her lips as she took in all the minute details of the imposing structure. If there really was a rebel faction, they must be hiding out in there. This was the place she'd been searching for.

Now she just needed to find them. A little voice in the back of her head told her that it wouldn't be too hard.

Sariah strode up to the giant door-like frame at the entrance to the fortress and looked for a knocker or some other way of signaling someone, but she found nothing.

She rolled her eyes. This might be harder than she thought. She placed a hand on the wood, gingerly at first, then she applied more pressure, hoping to push the door open. Of course, it didn't budge.

"Hello?" she called out. Her voice echoed in the shadows of the massive structure.

There was no response. She tried knocking a few times, but that had a similar result. In frustration, she kicked the door once with her injured foot, then immediately regretted it as a fresh jolt of pain shot up her leg, making her feel a little ill.

Sariah slumped to the ground and put her back to the door. Maybe it was pointless, she thought, and this place was just as empty as it looked.

Just as she was about to get up and start walking away, she heard someone grumbling nearby.

"Who goes there?" a gruff voice demanded. Sariah turned to see who was talking to her, but couldn't see anyone. The sun was in a bad spot, and it blinded her temporarily. She hastily put a hand over her eyes and tried to focus.

"Just a humble traveler looking for protection from the elements," she said in a voice barely over a whisper.

"You'll find no shelter here," the voice told her. "You'd

best turn around and go back from whence you came, young one."

Sariah was a little incensed at some disembodied voice referring to her as a "young one," but she knew better than to challenge it. She got up and stepped back from the door a little bit. Once she was a few feet back, she could see the head of a man peeking out from a window in the guard-house to the left of the wooden door.

It was hard to make out his features, but he looked surprisingly old with wisps of white hair tumbling out of his helmet and a hook-shaped nose sticking out of the front.

"Please sir, my friends told me I could come here. That you'd accept me."

Hook-nose huffed. "And who might those friends be, exactly?"

Sariah thought fast. Could she trust this person? He was in the right place, and he didn't look like a typical Dusk Raven. She decided that she could. "Valerie, my lord. A dress merchant from the city of Stratton. She said I could find you here."

The older man scowled. "Pfft. A name and a town you could have heard anywhere. Don't prove nothin'."

Sariah groaned. "Please, sir. I don't have much left. I was told you guys would help me. I'm here to help the fight against the Dusk Ravens." She took in a deep breath and bit her lip as she decided just how much to share. "Against...Gabriel."

There was a slight look of recognition in Hook-nose's eyes as they went wide. All at once, it was gone and his expression was neutral. The old man shrugged. "Ain't never heard of him."

"Oh, come on!" Sariah squealed. "I saw that flash of recognition! You know what I'm talking about! Please, you're all I've got left."

Hook-nose looked at her with eyes full of pity for a second, then he shook his head. "I'm sorry, miss, but rules are rules. Run along now." With that, he turned and slunk back into the shadows.

"Wait!" Sariah cried after him. "I can prove it!" Her mind raced. What was that phrase Valerie had told her to repeat? She just had to remember it—something about an eagle.

It came to her. "The eagle has risen over the hills!"

The old man stopped in his tracks, and his shoulders hiked up. Slowly, he turned and returned to the window. "What was that my dear?" he asked. His tone was much softer than it had been earlier.

"I said, 'the eagle has risen over the hills.'"

Hook-nose rubbed his chin for a moment. "Hmm, I suppose you might be telling the truth after all," he said thoughtfully. "Sorry for the gruff demeanor. Can't be too careful these days, you understand."

Sariah nodded. That she could agree with completely. "Then you'll help me?"

Hook-nose chuckled. "I'll let you in the front door. The rest is up to you. Now, you might want to stand back."

Her nose wrinkled, and she cocked her head to the side. "Stand back?" she repeated.

It didn't take Sariah long to figure out why. A moment

later, the ground underneath her rumbled as the giant door started opening from the top down.

Sariah scrambled backward and marveled at the bizarre device. Who came up with these strange inventions, anyway? she thought.

Before she could do anything else, Hook-nose emerged and strode over the now-open door, which had nestled quite nicely into the ground beneath him. He stood slightly hunched over and looked at her expectantly, arms out in front of him.

"Ahem," he said, clearing his throat. "Welcome, my dear, to Talon's Reach."

***

Will felt an itch coming on. It was creeping up his back something fierce, begging to be dealt with. Still, he was in the presence of their leader, and he couldn't do anything about it now. He'd just have to suck it up.

He looked past Ilene, their leader, into the center of the courtyard. A small young woman, perhaps sixteen or seventeen years of age, stood in front of them. On her back was a pack that was entirely too small to have let her make the voyage out here, and at her side rested a sword that looked altogether too big for her tiny hands.

Will snorted. He leaned in close to Ilene. "I don't like it," he whispered in her ear.

Ilene tilted her head gently in his direction. "What don't you like?"

He nodded briefly at the girl. "Doesn't fit, I tell you. Something's wrong."

Ilene's lips curled upward into a smile. "Well, then we'll deal with her like we always do, won't we?"

Now it was Will's turn to smile. He backed away from Ilene, stood straighter and glowered at their guest. She would provide a satisfactory answer for her existence, or she would pay the price. Such was their way. He was good with that.

"Welcome to our humble home," Ilene said in a graceful tone. She beckoned toward the small girl with her hands. "Come closer so that we may inspect you properly."

Sariah took a hesitant step forward, then stopped. Her eyes were darting around wildly, looking at everyone around her instead of straight ahead.

Will huffed. Her head was in the wrong place—another thing to dislike about her.

Ilene smiled down at Sariah. "What is your name, child?"

"S-sariah, my lady," she answered with a slight stutter.

"Where do you come from?"

The young girl looked straight at Ilene for the first time. Will thought he caught a sense of awe in them, but it faded quickly. "I hail from Chatwick, a small mining town not far from here," the girl related.

Ilene nodded. "Very well. Tell me, how did you hear about us?"

"Valerie, the dress merchant in Stratton, confided your existence to me," Sariah answered matter-of-factly.

Will's eyes narrowed. Valerie had vouched for this whelp? Valerie never vouched for anyone. It was obviously a well-manicured lie. He leaned in close to whisper as much into Ilene's ear, but she waved him off.

"What brings you here, child?" Ilene continued without skipping a beat. "Or put a different way, why should we answer your plea for help?"

Sariah knelt on the ground and bowed her head slightly, then raised it. She began speaking, relaying the sordid tale of her adventures up to this point, and leaving nothing out.

Once or twice during the tale, Will saw Ilene's eyes widen in surprise. She gave no other indication that the story was anything but ordinary. He admired her composure for the hundredth time. She was an amazing leader.

He was less than convinced. As far as he was concerned, this Sariah girl was utterly unimpressive, and her story was obviously greatly embellished. There was no way that little slip of a thing could have felled two of the Dusk Raven's finest on her own.

Will spat on the ground and ignored the rest of Sariah's speech. The girl was a liar, and she deserved a liar's death. He found Ilene's next words shocking.

"Your voyage must have been a hard one to come all the way out here alone," their leader said. She lowered her head slightly to look into Sariah's eyes a little easier. "We will help you, my child."

Will's eyes filled with rage. "How could you! She's a fat liar, she is!" he spat. He had tried to keep his words in check, but he was unable to stay quiet any longer. This was going too far. Ilene was being deceived by a common liar.

Ilene's eyes narrowed, and she glared at him. She spoke to him with a cold, reprimanding tone. "I will not tolerate outbursts in my court." Her tone was firm and unrelenting.

Will lowered his head. He knew he'd acted out of line. "Sorry, Mistress Ilene." He slunk back a half step.

Ilene gave him a wry, knowing smile, then wiped it from her face and turned back toward their visitor.

"Thank you, mistress!" Sariah said then. A broad smile played across her face.

The crowd around them erupted into a chorus of noise, half-cheers, half-demands for her to be sent away. Ilene held up one finger to her lips, calling for silence. Both the crowd and the visitor girl looked suitably reprimanded and lowered their heads in shame.

"We will help you, dearie," Ilene repeated, "if you can pass our initiation challenge. You will face a trial by combat to prove your worth. Worry not, it shall be a fair trial. Such is our way, and if you aim to seek our help, you must follow in our ways."

Sariah lifted her head. "And if I refuse to participate?"

A collective "ooh" ran through the crowd, and several people shook their heads in disapproval.

"Then you will not leave here alive." Ilene's voice displayed no sign of emotion as she spoke the damning words.

Sariah seemed lost in thought for several minutes, then she nodded. "Very well. I accept your terms."

Another cheer ran through the crowd, with more joining in than had before.

Ilene's lips curled upward just a bit, showing a hint of a long tooth on one side. "Good. The combat trial goes until the drawing of first blood. Win, and we will give you the aid you seek and accept you as one of our own. Lose, and you will gain nothing, but you will be allowed to leave freely so long as you vow to never return." She paused for just a moment to let the words sink in. "Do you understand, my child?"

Sariah gave a firm nod. "I do."

More rumblings came from the crowd. Most of them seemed to be of the approving sort, though there were a few scoffs as well.

"Excellent." Ilene clapped her hands together, then turned to look at Will. A mischievous smile flashed across her lips. "Will, please do me the honor of administering the test."

At last, it was his turn to prove the truth of his words. He grinned at Ilene, then spared a pitying glance at their little visitor. The poor girl would never know what hit her.

"With pleasure."

CHAPTER FIVE

The man known only as the Master roamed the hallways of his complex. He was in a bit of a sour mood today, but he was trying his best not to show it.

Not that anyone could have noticed, anyway. He was disguised, as always. Today he had donned the appearance of a tall, thin female with short brown hair. The girl had a small tattoo of a dragon running down one arm. It was mostly covered by the oversized brown tunic he was wearing. The appearance was otherwise completely unremarkable.

He thought briefly of the mess he'd left back in his study. There was a pile of paperwork a mile high sitting on his desk, waiting for his attention. He sighed. It seemed that empires always ran on a sea of paperwork.

The Master didn't relish the thought of returning to paperwork, as necessary as it was. He'd been forced to kill the servant who had brought it to him. The poor sop's body was now bleeding out all over his expensive carpet. Stains like that would probably never come out.

The fool had kept droning on and on about trade deals and why they just had to be signed today. He did not see that the Master was already in a foul mood and not wanting to be bothered with such paltry details. He just hoped there weren't any bloodstains on any of the papers. Some of the more squeamish parties affixed to those deals would be alarmed to see blood and might assume the worst.

The only real downside was that now he had another body to clean up. And a new rug to purchase, of course. It was the cost of doing business, he supposed. There was nothing he could do about it now.

He made a mental note to send in another servant to deal with the mess. It would serve a dual purpose—the cleanup would be handled, and the new servant would know what his future held if he ever acted the same way.

The Master smiled. He liked it when things worked out nice and neat like that.

Humming softly to himself, he kept walking through the winding hallways. He was headed toward his lab. On days like today, only his lab could make him happy.

Though lately, even the comforts offered there were wearing on him. If he didn't make another breakthrough in his research soon, he simply didn't know what he'd do.

Is my quest impossible? he wondered.

The Master shook his head. It seemed unlikely. He had yet to find a limit to the magic powers the nanocytes granted him. He was sure what he sought was attainable. He just had to figure out how to call it forth.

He rounded another bend and finally came to the door he was looking for. From the outside, it looked like any other in the complex. No one could tell the kinds of horrors that went on just a few feet beyond the wooden barrier.

The Master knocked, then briefly wondered why he bothered. It wasn't like he really expected an answer from his prisoners.

"Who is it?" a strained voice said from within. It sounded broken and tired, with a tinge of pain.

The Master smiled. He turned the doorknob and let the door swing wide. Taking a few steps into the room, he turned on the magitech lights lining the walls, then closed the door.

His victim winced at the sudden light after having spent some time alone in the dark and closed his eyes.

The Master walked over to the man chained against the wall. He took out one finger and gently caressed the man's cheek with it. A shiver erupted across the man's body, and he shook involuntarily. The Master caught a whiff of something sour and looked down to see a dark, wet spot on the man's pants.

He shook his head slightly and tsked. This one wasn't made of hearty stock like many of his other victims. He'd need to find a way to get better recruits again. That was no small feat, seeing as he was starting to run out of promising students.

The Master leaned in close to his victim's ear and started to whisper. "We don't have much time. We have to hurry," he said in a feminine voice. He added a sense of urgency to the tone for good measure.

The man chained to the wall seemed shocked to hear a woman's voice. Slowly, he pried open his eyes and looked at the Master, who looked like a simple servant girl. The prisoner's face softened, and he stopped shaking as hard.

"Can you loosen these chains?" the prisoner asked. His voice was shaky, but it was starting to firm up.

The Master nodded. "I think so. Let me see." He started toying with the chains on the walls, running his hands up and down and shaking them for effect.

"Hurry!" the prisoner exclaimed. There was still a good bit of fear in his eyes, but a slight hint of hope, too.

A smile crept across the Master's lips. He so liked it when his victims thought they had a chance of survival. It made crushing those hopes so much more fun in the end. "I've almost got it," he said.

The Master played with the chains for another moment to make it look like he was working them loose, then finally flicked a tiny switch on the wall and they came undone. "Got it!" he shouted.

His prisoner grinned at him. He rubbed his wrists where the shackles had dug into them. "Thank you!" the man said. His voice was firmer, and there was a good bit of hope in his eyes.

All the better to crush, the Master thought coolly.

He looked around like he thought they were in danger and spoke in a hushed tone. "Come, let's get out of here before anyone notices you're missing," he told the prisoner.

"I'll lead the way," the prisoner offered, nodding. "Follow me."

The Master smiled up at him and beckoned for him to take the lead. The prisoner ran toward the door and flung it open. He took a last look at his poor unsuspecting savior, then closed the door, locking it in the same motion.

Shaking his head, the Master sighed and thunked his hand against his forehead. They were always the same, his prisoners, thinking of themselves and never of others.

So predictable.

He waited a moment, then he walked over to the door and opened it. The locking mechanism was a fake, so the door slid open easily. Walking into the hallway, he looked at his prisoner, who was sprawled on the floor, dazed and undoubtedly very confused.

It was his favorite trick. Let them think they're escaping, then have them run headfirst into an invisible wall of energy. It worked every time.

"Tsk, tsk," the Master said with a shake of his head. He was speaking in his normal voice now. "Come now, we must get you back to your place of honor."

Reaching out with one of his currently dainty-looking hands, he grabbed his prisoner by the shoulder. The man was dazed, and his head rolled as the Master dragged his body. Hitting that invisible wall head-first had done quite a number on him.

It didn't matter. He didn't need to be in tip-top shape.

He gave the big man another tug. His weight was immense, most of it from fat with a little muscle thrown about here and there. Whoever this Charles used to be, he must have led a good life and a pampered existence. Which made the fact of his end all the more exciting.

But first, he had to get the man back in place before he came to or start all over again. He spared a glance at his time-keeping device. It was half-past the lunch hour already. If he didn't hurry, he wouldn't be able to finish before supper.

With a groan and a giant shove, he managed to get his victim into the lab and propped back up against the wall. The Master reached with one hand while steadying Charles with the other and grabbed a manacle. From there, it was a simple matter of re-attachment.

For a moment, he thought about securing both manacles. Charles would be in more pain this way, so he left the man only half-strung up.

The Master took a half step back and looked over his subject. A big, purple bruise was starting to form near the man's temple. It must be what had taken the sense out of the man. His head was hanging down at a bit of an odd angle, and his eyes were closed.

It seemed that his prisoner wouldn't be waking from that injury any time soon. He so loved to talk to his victims as he worked, too. This simply wouldn't do. The only solution was that he'd have to heal the man first.

He let out a deep sigh and placed a hand gently on the man's head. Healing energy flowed from his fingertips into the wound. Within seconds, the bruising and swelling dissipated, replaced with tight, soft skin.

The work only took a few seconds, but it left the Master feeling slightly drained. Now he just needed to wait and see whether it would be worth it.

A few moments later, his victim's eyes started to stir. The man lifted his head up slightly, then blinked a few times. The Master's lips curled into a half-smile. It was working.

Still, time was wasting. He slapped Charles across the face. The bewildered man shook his head and opened his eyes fully to greet the new threat.

The sight that awaited the now-wakened Charles likely shocked the poor man to his core. The female that had been there earlier was gone, replaced with someone who probably looked oddly familiar to him. "M-master?" the man's shaky voice asked with a stutter.

"Yes, my child, it is I," the Master replied. He placed one hand gently underneath the man's chin and lifted his face so he could stare into Charles's eyes. "I am here to grant you your salvation, Charles," he added with a grin.

He had dropped his illusion so the man could look at the Master's actual face. It was easier to concentrate when he didn't have to keep up appearances, so he often abandoned his disguises while working in his lab. Of course, that meant that no one could leave alive, which had never been a problem.

Charles got to whimpering. It was obvious the poor man didn't know how to handle pain or tense situations very well, and at the moment, he had heaps of both.

The Master tsked again and shook his head. The Charles before him might have looked strong physically, but deep down, he was just as weak as the rest of them. What a pity.

"Please, M-master. I'll...I'll d-do anything," Charles said between sobs.

"Now Charles," the Master started. He let out another sigh. "You know this is for your own good. Please don't take offense. It's just business, you understand."

More whimpers came, and an awful stench far worse than before. Has Charles soiled himself again? the Master wondered. It seemed likely. He'd have his servants clean it up later, along with the body.

The Master plugged his nose and let his hands trail up and down Charles's naked, hairy chest in an absent-minded fashion.

"Oh, Charles," he said. "You really had no idea, did you?"

Charles merely whimpered in reply and didn't move. This was getting ridiculous.

The Master continued, ignoring the man's weak noises. "Do you know the one big drawback of using magic, Charles?"

Charles shook his head slightly but said nothing. The look of abject fear was back in his eyes.

"Of course you do, Charles. Come now, even my youngest students know this bit," the Master insisted. "If I recall correctly, you'd done quite well in the lower classes. A shame you never passed on to the higher levels."

The Master continued. "The main drawback is that it weakens you. The nanocytes take their energy from your own body to fuel the magic. Even the strongest magic users get weak and tired from prolonged use. It's an unfortunate limitation to an otherwise wondrous gift. But alas, everything must have a downside, right Charles?"

"B-b-beg pardon?" Charles asked with a look of confusion.

The Master waved him off. "Oh come now, you remember this part. Don't play coy with me." He took another hard look at Charles, but the man still seemed confused and despondent. "Anyway, think about it for just a moment. Imagine if there was a way to keep from getting tired, and keep the weakness at bay. To keep using magic beyond what one human would normally be capable of?"

The Master's eyes grew big as saucers and there was a

gleam in them as he went on. "Why, Charles, such a man would be nigh on unstoppable. Of course, there's no way that power such as that could come from within. We've already covered that. The body's energy stores are inherently limited. So naturally, I had to look outside myself to find that extra source of power. To others, if you will."

Charles' expression changed as the poor man pondered the Master's words. His face went from greater confusion to acknowledgment, and finally, one of terror as he started to understand his purpose in this sordid affair.

"Yes." The Master nodded. "You get it now. If I could pull the energy out of other people, I could use it to augment my own stores and never grow tired. I would never experience that drawback."

He paused for a second. "Now I know what you're thinking, dearie. Such a feat must surely be impossible. And yet, healing—sending one's energy willfully into another to repair their body—that works. So why not the reverse as well?" His smile grew even broader. "At least, that's my theory, anyway."

The Master's voice trailed off, and he seemed lost in thought. Then he turned his attention back to Charles and clapped his hands together. "Let's see if it works, shall we?"

Charles let a small cry escape his lips. It was barely audible and was as weak as the man who offered it.

The Master shook his head again. "Now that simply won't do at all. Let's work on that scream of yours, too, shall we?"

Without warning, the Master fanned out his fingers on his right hand and shoved it forward hard enough to dig his nails into Charles' chest. Then, he started chanting the words to a spell.

A terrible wave of energy washed over poor Charles, and the man's insides started twisting in odd ways. The scream that escaped him was profound as blood began seeping from the man's very pores.

The Master's eyes glinted in the magitech light, and his smile grew even broader. He kept working on Charles, trying to force the man's nanocytes to bend to his will.

For a moment, he felt like the whole thing was finally working. Then all at once, Charles fell silent, and his head flopped against his chest.

The Master frowned. Dead already? he thought. This Charles really was a weakling.

He took a few steps back and sat down on a chair, ready to nurse the headache that always followed these experiments. Only this time, the headache never came. He sat up, then, and stretched out his muscles. They didn't feel anywhere near as weak or rubbery as they usually did after an intense casting session.

Was it because Charles had expired so fast? Or was there more to it?

He wondered if his hard work had finally paid off, and he had finally unraveled the secret to the spell. It was possible, he supposed. He'd need more test subjects to really know for sure. Those were getting harder to come by these days.

He had to know for sure.

A knock at the door to his lab roused him from his thoughts. The Master sighed and rolled his eyes. Hastily, he put on a disguise. It wasn't much, just a simple robed figure with a slight hunch in his back. It seemed appropriate, given the circumstances.

"Come in," the Master called. The door creaked and grated on its hinges as it swung open to reveal two servants carrying an unconscious girl between them.

The Master's eyes brightened again. "Ah, good, I see you've found me another willing participant. And sooner than I thought."

One of the servants nodded, but neither said anything.

"Chain her up over there on the far wall, please," he said, motioning to a set of manacles across from him.

There was another nod, but no words. His servants were remarkably well-behaved today. He'd have to reward them with extra treats later. As cruel as he could be, he always rewarded good behavior. It kept them from rebellion.

"Oh, and when you're done with that, please come clean up this mess over here." He pointed to Charles's dead body and the awful stain on the floor. "It seems poor Charles here couldn't hold it together very well."

His servants got to work. He stepped over a pile of something smelly and sticky, vomit maybe, and walked over to his latest victim, and waited. A few minutes later, the mess and the smell were gone, and he was alone in his lab again, with only the girl.

The Master spoke a few words and woke the girl from her slumber. She stared at him wild-eyed. There was a fierceness to her eyes that hadn't been there in Charles. It was almost like this one still had some fight left.

Another smile crossed his lips, this one brighter than before. A fighter was a refreshing change of pace.

With one clawed hand, he firmly gripped the woman's chin and pulled it toward him. She fought but was ultimately helpless to do anything about it.

"Good afternoon, Charles," he said to her. "We're going to have such a lovely time this afternoon, just the two of us. I can hardly wait to begin."

Gabriel stepped in something and scowled. He looked down at his foot. It was covered in a substance that looked like mud but smelled far worse. He wrinkled his nose in disgust and did his best to wipe it away on a dry patch of ground, then kept going.

He cast an invisibility spell and started toward the gates of Stratton. A wry grin crossed his face. The object of his ire would soon be snuffed out.

As he neared the gates, he huffed slightly at the line of people waiting to be let in, knowing they could neither see nor hear his presence. His mission being what it was, he quite preferred it that way.

He knew the gate guard, Sergeant Ty would let him through fast and proper if he asked. The man was a good soldier, his loyalty bought ages ago, but he had no time for that today. He still would have had to go through the queue like one of the other peasants. It was much better this way and cleaner, too.

Gabe passed by the gate quickly, no one sparing a glance in his direction. He sauntered on through and made his way to the fountain. Once there, he hid behind the massive statue in the middle and removed his invisibility spell. He made his presence known slowly to keep from surprising anyone who might have caught even a hint of his movement.

He'd thought about leaving the invisibility spell on until his mission was complete but had quickly disregarded the idea. That would have drained his resources, and he wanted to be fully alert when it came time to do the deed.

It wouldn't have done him any good in Market Square anyway. The place was crawling with so many people, it would have done him more harm to not be visible.

Groaning a little, Gabe turned toward Market Square and surveyed the crowds. They were heavier than average. Something special must be going on in the market today.

He wondered if it was a holiday, not that it mattered. He wasn't there for the crowds.

Gabe strode forward, his head low, determined as he crashed through the throngs of people. He was headed toward a particular stall in the back. Every time he came across someone standing too long in one spot or otherwise blocking his way, he'd scowl at them. His gaze was such that no one wanted to mess with him, and everybody gave him a wide berth.

The corner of one of his lips curled upward slightly into an almost-snarl at how powerful it made him feel. It felt good to remember that he was better than them. Things were as they should be.

Within a few minutes, he made his way through the crowds and saw his destination—Valerie's tent.

His expression soured, and he clenched his fists tight enough that his nails left red marks on his skin. It took him a few moments to unclench them and calm down enough to think straight.

Here it is, he thought. She'll wish she'd never seen me.

He contemplated setting the whole tent ablaze without ever entering. It would be quick and clean, but not satisfying. He wouldn't get to watch that bitch squirm and scream in pain.

He needed to do this personally.

Slowly, he walked forward. He watched for any signs of movement from within to make sure she didn't run off and hide.

The corner of his eye caught sight of a lovely red dress, and it gave him pause. It looked just like the one Sariah had worn on their little date. The memory brought a tear to his eye.

What am I doing? he pondered. In that moment of clarity, he knew it wasn't the dress merchant he was mad at. Not really. She had played a part, yes, but only a part. He had some responsibility for what had happened too.

For the briefest second, his resolve faltered. Then it returned in a rush, and his anger flared to life again. Who was he kidding? He was pissed at her! Valerie died today!

With an evil grin, he stormed into the tent, throwing the flaps wide and knocking over a few mannequins in the process. Bits of wood and cloth rolled in every direction, making a gigantic mess.

Gabe looked everywhere, but the stall was empty. Somehow, his quarry had escaped him. He let out a long, deep scream and let his anger at the situation wash over him. He felt the need to lash out magically and let the feeling consume him. It felt good to let it all go and allow the magic wash over him.

White-hot ropes of fire erupted from his body in every direction and engulfed everything they touched. In the dry heat of the day, the delicate fabrics were destroyed in seconds.

Soon, it was over and he found himself kneeling in the dirt, surrounded by ashes. Valerie's tent was destroyed, as were several other tents around it.

Somewhere behind him, the fire still raged. People were rushing in with buckets to try and stop the blaze before it consumed the whole of Market Square, but it looked like it would all be for naught. The blaze, like his hatred, was unstoppable.

Gabe watched people scurry to and fro for a few moments, then donned his invisibility spell again and walked away.

Today had been disappointing, but it was only a setback. Valerie would still pay for what she'd done. He'd make sure of it.

While the peasants fought to stop the fire, he turned and left Stratton as unseen and unceremoniously as he'd entered. He needed information, and he thought he knew just where to find it.

CHAPTER SIX

Sariah felt a knot form in her gut. She looked at the warrior standing across from her. The man known as Will towered over her menacingly.

He was surprisingly intimidating. Tall, like Harvey and Gabe—maybe a hair taller, even. Unlike them, he had a very slender build, though she could see his muscles straining against the fabric of his tunic. His black hair hung in little rivulets around his neck, and he had some fresh stubble on his face like he was a few days overdue for a good shave.

Will grinned at her, and she could see his teeth were in remarkably good condition. All told, she guessed the man was around twenty years old, maybe a little older. He wasn't much older than her but looked like he'd spent those years training harder than she ever had.

She wasn't sure what she had gotten herself into.

She didn't know what good could come from this little competition, or what information her new allies were hoping to glean. They didn't need to put her up against an opponent that obviously outclassed her completely to prove she knew how to carry a sword. Still, she'd signed up for it willingly enough, and she was determined not to lose.

She noticed Will hadn't reached for his weapon yet and wondered why. Not wanting to be caught unawares, she reached for her own sword at her side and pulled it from her sheath.

Will glanced down at her blade and held one hand out in front of him. "Hold right there," he said. His voice was melodic. In any other situation, she probably would have swooned over it. But right now, not a chance in hell.

Sariah bit her lip. Was this a trick meant to catch her off guard? After Will didn't move for several more seconds, she supposed it wasn't. She lowered her blade.

Her opponent nodded once. "Good. We'll not use the longer blades for this. Too dangerous," he explained. "Daggers and fists only."

She nodded and set her sword on the ground some distance away from her. She didn't need to trip on it later. Will did the same with his own blade. Someone came by and took both of them, ostensibly so they couldn't reach for them during combat.

Though she felt slightly naked without her trusty sword, there wasn't much she could do about it. Inwardly, she was glad Gabe had made her study some knife moves, too.

Who knew they'd come in handy so soon?

The big man across from her nodded at someone else in the crowd, still holding his hand in front of him. A person dressed in white robes came through the crowd that had formed around them.

Sariah looked around and noticed the throng of people now standing around the two of them in a wide arc. Some were hooting and hollering, others whispering and exchanging coins in what were most likely wagers.

At that moment, it felt like everyone in the whole city had come to watch her. The attention only increased her tension.

The white-robed figure took a few steps forward and closed the distance between them, his hands held out in front of him as well. He reached one hand out to Sariah, and she flinched backward involuntarily.

White Robe grinned at her. "This won't hurt a bit, miss," he said in a soothing voice. "Might feel good, actually." He touched her very gently, and she felt a warming sensation wash over her. It was all at once comforting and familiar. The man was healing her. But why?

"We want to make sure you're at your best," Will said then as if answering her question.

She nodded once. She supposed that made sense. They didn't want anyone to be able to blame a loss on not being in a good state of health.

White Robe withdrew his fingers then and walked back into the crowd. Sariah had to admit she was feeling pretty good about then. She tested the foot she'd injured on the way in. It was free of pain.

"Do you need a weapon?" Will asked her.

Sariah shook her head. "No, I have a dagger of my own."

He inclined his head. "Let's see it, then."

She reached under her tunic and took out the dagger she always carried with her, Lucien's dagger. It felt wrong somehow to use it here, but at least she was familiar with it. Fighting with an unfamiliar blade would put her at a disadvantage.

A collective gasp rocked through the crowd as she brought her dagger forth. It seemed they, too, knew it had once been the blade of Lucien. Or someone high up in the Dusk Raven order, at least.

Will's eyes glowered, and he practically spat at her. "Get that from your lover, did you?" he sneered.

The implication incensed her, and Sariah lunged forward, intent on ending the combat quickly. She made a quick, low swipe with her blade that Will easily dodged.

Panting a little from the failed action, she withdrew, though she didn't take her eyes off of Will.

He gave off a low whistle. "Careful now, dearie. You could hurt yourself with that thing."

Sariah's cheeks grew red, and she wanted to swipe at him again, but then she realized he hadn't even pulled his own blade yet.

What game was he playing? she thought, cocking her head to the side.

Then it hit her. The big man didn't even consider her a threat. He probably thought she'd fall on her face as soon as swing a real weapon.

Her cheeks flushed, and her temper flared higher. She went at him again, swiping high and low, but he moved deftly out of the way at the last minute and swatted her hard on the back with an open palm. The suddenness of the blow sent her sprawling.

Sariah's face smashed hard into the dirt with an audible thud. Slowly, she got up onto her knees. Her face felt raw and bruised, and she thought a tooth might be loose, but she had no time to worry about it.

Looking over at Will, she saw him doing a sort of bow to the crowd, now cheering him on, and lapping up the attention.

Sariah scowled at herself, then got to her feet and dusted off her breeches. The big man had wanted to get under her skin, and she'd let him walk right in like he owned her. She blushed a little in embarrassment, then took a second to calm her nerves.

I can do this, she told herself. She inhaled deeply and returned her focus to her opponent. When Will finally turned back to her, she was in a better place, and she gave him a look filled with fierce determination.

"Draw your blade, sir," she called over to him. "Let's start this thing for real."

Will's face broke into a wide grin. "About time you showed up," he said dismissively. But he pulled out his own dagger all the same.

"I'm going to enjoy this," Will told her.

Sariah smiled back at him. "Oh, I don't think you will."

Will lurched forward, leading with his left foot and hand, lunging for Sariah's midsection. A quick swipe across her middle would end this charade nice and quick.

But Sariah's blade smashed into his own at the last second, deflecting the blow.

He scowled. The little girl had gotten lucky. It wouldn't hold.

She came at him then with a vertical swipe of her own, but he dodged back quickly enough. He could read her moves quite clearly. Whoever had trained her had done a good job, but he was better.

He came at her with another swipe aimed below her guard. This time he came in faster, but she managed to dodge out of the way at the last second.

Will's maneuver left his flank open, and she pounced on it, blade out in front. He'd been prepared and twisted so that she went past him instead.

As she went flying past him, he stuck out his dagger and flicked at the exact right moment. The blade sliced into the fabric of her shirt, cutting it wide open, but finding no purchase in the delicate skin beneath it.

The move earned him more cheers from the crowd, and their energy fed him, making him swell with pride.

Will let out a grunt. So close.

Much to the girl's credit, she recovered quickly. He turned around to see her blade inches from his face. He recoiled but managed to stay away from the tip while she righted herself.

Some of the crowd let out cheers for Sariah after that maneuver. Apparently, they were a fickle bunch. Not that he cared that much.

This might be a little harder than he thought, he mused. But still, she was just a girl. He had this.

With lightning-quick reflexes, he lunged forward, aiming low. Most people had trouble guarding their legs, especially with such short weapons.

He made two quick swipes at her legs. One of them cut through her pant leg, but again nothing came of it.

It seemed her small size was actually working in her favor. There was so little of her it was hard to make direct contact.

He saw her blade coming at him from above, then, and he had to dodge to the side quickly, bringing his blade up at the last moment to keep hers from succeeding.

The action made him tumble forward into the dirt because of the odd angle of movement, but he went into a roll and ended up back on his feet.

Someone in the crowd gawked at him, and a few more cheers for Sariah erupted from the bunch.

Will glowered, half at the girl and half at the stupid crowd. If they weren't careful, he'd have his way with the lot of them, too, when this was over.

Besides, he had Sariah's number now and knew how to win this thing. She was good. Better than he'd thought, even. But not good enough.

He took another few furtive swipes at her midsection, and she blocked them easily enough, but he expected that. He was just trying to wear her down a bit before he went in for the kill. Maybe he'd win back the crowd a bit.

Just then, he noticed a second blade appear in the girl's hand. He saw the dagger flying toward him just in time for him to knock it out of the air with his own.

The action sent him backward a half-step, and he had to right himself after.

A few gasps erupted from the crowd. This time it was understandable.

He scowled at the girl. Two daggers against his one was unsportsmanlike! He mentally shrugged. 'Twas a dirty trick, but it wasn't against the rules. Besides, now she no longer held that advantage.

Will came at her with a broad swipe to force her backward. He sliced at her gut once, then again at her feet. It had the desired effect. She retreated.

As he advanced, he swept up her spare dagger with his free hand. Now it was his turn to have a little fun.

More cheers came now, once again for him. His smile broadened, and his chest swelled again.

Will went in for a high swipe with one of the daggers, then followed it up with another a bit lower. Sariah dodged both strikes but fell backward doing so.

That made the crowd erupt like madmen.

He let out a low growl. She was his now.

Sariah started to get up, but he kicked her with one of his feet and sent her back to the ground. Then, he knelt next to her.

"I've got you now, you little chump," he spat at her. Then he raised his dagger in his right hand and made a wide swipe.

He expected to hear the satisfying sound of flesh parting as he sliced her arm open, but heard nothing.

The sudden silence of the crowd unnerved him more than anything, and he looked in their direction.

"What's wrong?" No answer came from the fickle spectators, only mild awe and a few finger-pointers.

Turning his attention back to the girl on the ground, his face quickly soured.

He blinked a few times in shock. Sariah was gone. She'd not only dodged the blow but disappeared entirely!

Sariah drew a deep breath to calm herself. She was invisible. At the last second, she'd rolled away and cast the spell, not sure what else to do.

Will was clearly more well versed in the art of dagger-wielding. Once he'd managed to get ahold of her spare blade, she knew the end was coming fast. Casting the invisibility spell had been something of a last resort. She'd been hesitant to do it, but her other option had been losing pathetically.

And she wasn't about to lose.

She watched Will scurry about on the ground a bit, looking dumbfounded. From her relatively safe position, it was kind of funny to watch.

He got up, then, his eyes looking in every direction. "Come out, you stupid wench!" he cried. He swung his daggers in front of him in wide arcs.

Sariah wanted to giggle, but if she was honest with herself, she was kind of cheating. Still, no one had said she couldn't do it.

With practiced ease, she crept up behind him. Once she was inches away, she let go of her spell.

The crowd hissed at Will, and he spun around quickly. But Sariah was ready. She swiped at him with Lucien's blade, and it bit into the exposed flesh of Will's arm as he spun around to face her.

She looked down at the blade triumphantly. It had the tiniest hint of Will's blood on the tip. She'd scored no more than a glancing blow, but she'd done it all the same.

A smile spread across her face, and she held up the

blade for the crowd to see. They cheered her name loudly, seemingly suitably impressed.

"I win," she told Will, grinning at him like an idiot.

Will's gaze went first to her blade, then to his injured arm, and finally to her. He scowled and threw her dagger at her hilt-first. "Cheater!" he quipped. "Come at me again without your tricks and see how you fare!"

She shrugged and shook her head. "You'd like that, wouldn't you? But rules are rules. I still won."

The man's cheeks burned red, and it looked like he was about to explode. "Listen here, you little witch! You cheated! You should feel lucky you're still alive."

He advanced on her then, and she backed away until she butted up against someone in the crowd.

Will loomed over her, his dagger held menacingly close to her face. He spoke and practically spat on her at the same time. "Yeah, that's what I thought. Nothing but a coward when the chips are down. Wouldn't fare that well in real combat, would you, you little bitch?"

His blade inched closer to her throat, and she gulped down hard as bile rose in the back of her throat. No one in the crowd seemed willing to stop him. In fact, they were cheering him on.

Sariah closed her eyes and wondered if this was it. She supposed there were worse ways to go. At least he wasn't a Dusk Raven.

"Stop!" an icy voice called over the crowd. Instantly, Will's blade fell, clattering forgotten to the floor.

The big man backed away from her then and held his hands up, as did the rest of the crowd.

Sariah looked to see who had issued the command and

demanded such respect. It was the leader of the group. The woman had a sour expression on her face that gave the impression she was not to be toyed with.

Will turned and looked at her. He bowed his head slightly. "Aww, Ilene, look. I didn't mean nothin' by it, I swear," he groveled.

Ilene leveled her gaze at him, and he got down on one knee and bowed his head further. She seemed satisfied by that.

Sariah was in awe that someone could command brutes like Will with just a look. Inwardly, she wanted to be like her one day. She smiled at her savior, but when Ilene's gaze fell on her, she gave her the same icy glare, and Sariah wiped the smile from her face, bowing her head to the woman as well.

Ilene walked forward and stopped in front of Will. She bade him rise. "Will," she said in that same icy tone. "Is there a rule forbidding the use of magic in the trial?"

Will shook his head slightly. "No," he croaked in barely a whisper. "I mean, no, my lady," he repeated loud enough for the crowd to hear.

"Then it would seem our visitor won fair and square, would it not?"

He cleared his throat. "Y-yes, my lady," he said, a sullen expression on his face. "But it wasn't fair! She disappeared!" he added in a whiny tone.

"Silence!" Ilene demanded. He shut up. "I saw the combat, same as you. I say she acted fairly." She looked up and scanned the crowd, meeting the eyes of everyone. "Does anyone here disagree?"

Sariah heard a few mutters and scraping feet, but

everyone in the crowd bowed their heads and said nothing. She wanted to snicker, but she kept her mouth shut.

Ilene nodded. "I thought not." She turned her attention to Sariah and smiled at her briefly. "Sorry for that earlier display of rudeness. I believe congratulations are in order."

The lady extended her hand. Sariah stared at it like she had no idea what to do, then finally she shook it. Ilene's hands were cold, like her voice. It was cool and freaky all at once.

Ilene flashed her another smile, and it felt warm and inviting, a stark contrast to the rest of her. "Welcome to the Eagle's Claw Clan," she said.

Sariah grinned at her. "Thank you," she replied. "So I passed, then? You'll help me?"

Ilene nodded once. "Yes, Sariah, you passed. There's just one more small matter to go over, and then it'll all be official."

Sariah groaned. Was there more? That fight hadn't been enough? What else could they possibly expect from her today?

But she swallowed it down. She'd come this far, and she would see it through the rest of the way. She nodded to Ilene once and tried to smile. "Of course, my...lady," she offered. The word felt odd on her tongue. "Whatever it takes."

The icy woman nodded. "It pleases us greatly to hear that. For that is how we live and operate here in the Eagle's Claw Clan. All that we have - our possessions, our talents, and skills, even our very lives, are not our own but rather the property of the clan. We all eat, sleep, and breathe the same mission - to see an end to the evil rule of the Dusk

Ravens. We recognize nothing short of full commitment will see us attain that goal."

Sariah nodded once. She could respect that level of determination and matched her own dedication to the cause.

Her heart felt a little lighter as she looked over Ilene and the crowd once again. She had made the right decision. These were her kind of people. She barely knew them, but with words like that, they already felt like family.

"I feel the same way, my lady," Sariah replied. "Like I said, whatever it takes."

The older woman clapped her hands together. "Excellent. You will surrender your belongings to the clan, then. Rest assured, you will be provided everything you should need when you need it, but personal possessions are foreign to us. Such is our way."

Sariah nodded. "But my lady, all I own are my clothes and my weapons. Surely I can keep those?"

Ilene's eyes darkened and she glared at her. Sariah felt a shiver run down her spine. "All possessions must be surrendered. Especially that." Her finger was pointing toward something on Sariah's breast.

She looked down to see what Ilene could possibly be pointing at. Was her tunic wide open or something? Then she saw it, the tiny brooch she always wore. It had little gemstones around the edges. It was the last memento she had from her parents. It was literally the only thing she had left of them.

Her mind raced and Sariah swallowed hard. Could she really give it up, her only bond to her dead parents? What choice did she have?

"It belonged to my parents." She knelt in front of Ilene and bowed her head, then looked up at her with pleading eyes. "Please, my lady, it's all I have left of them!"

Ilene shook her head gracefully. "I'm sorry, child, but at the market that brooch could also feed several children for a month. You must always think of the group and the greater good if you are to be one of us."

She gulped down hard. "Is…is there no other way?" Though she could understand the older woman's point of view, giving up her family heirloom seemed cruel to her, too.

The older woman lowered her gaze. "I am sorry, my child. I cannot make an exception for anyone. Such is our way."

Sariah took one last long, loving look at her brooch. She fingered it and thought about how her mother would fasten it to her blouse on Saint's day. She'd only worn it then, saying it was far too precious to be worn the rest of the year. Often, her mother had told Sariah it would one day be a wedding gift for her. It had seemed so precious then.

The memories of her mother brought a tear to her eye. She wiped it away quickly, not wanting to look weak in front of her new allies.

Looking the other way, she ripped the brooch off her shirt and held it out to Ilene. The woman's icy-cold hands briefly touched hers, and then the deed was done. It was gone. There was nothing of her past left now.

With tears streaming down her eyes, she looked up at Ilene. There was a tinge of sadness in the older woman's eyes as well.

At long last, Ilene spoke. Her voice was strong and carried over the entire ground to reach everyone's ears. "Today, we welcome a new member to our illustrious clan, the Eagle's Claw. Sariah has intimate knowledge of the Dusk Raven leadership. Today is a wondrous day, for today, our strength has grown!" She made a broad, sweeping motion with her hands to encompass the crowd. "Everyone, please welcome Sariah to our fold and do your best to make her feel at home."

Cheers erupted from every corner of the courtyard.

Sariah smiled. The pain in her chest from the loss of her brooch was quickly replaced with elation. At long last, she felt safe and happy in a way she hadn't in months. She recognized the feeling at once. She was home.

CHAPTER SEVEN

About two days had passed since the incident in the courtyard, and Sariah was starting to feel restless.

Ilene and the others had been most welcoming on that
first day. Well, most of the others. Will still seemed not to
like her much, but there were hundreds of people, so she
reckoned it would be pretty easy to avoid him most of the
time.

But the others had been very nice to her, answering her
questions and making her feel like one of them. She'd had
plenty of questions, too, like how their organization could
remain a secret even though there were so many of them.

"Carefully," Ilene had told her with a slight snicker. She
glowered as she remembered that conversation, all one
word of it. She would have to ask more pointed questions
in the future. Other than that incident, everyone had been
quite forthcoming.

Apparently, the Eagle's Claw Clan had been in operation for several years. Almost as long as the Dusk Ravens,
actually. They had several hundred members spread out all

over the place. Supposedly there was even a representative in Chatwick, though she had no idea who that could be. She thought she knew everyone in her old hometown too well for them to hide a secret like that.

She shook her head to clear the thought. It didn't really matter, she supposed.

A couple of times, she asked why they weren't more forthright in attacking the Dusk Ravens. Ilene had assured her that even though their numbers looked strong, the Dusk Ravens were still far stronger. That and the Dusk Ravens had far more members trained for magical combat.

There had been a few skirmishes in the past, but none of them had gone well. The Dusk Raven mages were just too strong for them.

She could understand that. She shivered as she remembered her encounter with Gabriel. The man had been an absolute monster. If the other Dusk Raven mages were even half his ability, she could understand the Eagle's Clan hesitation in engaging.

Instead, they bided their time and trained, growing their strength until such time they could actually do something with it.

Only biding one's time wasn't all that exciting. At least, not enough to keep Sariah busy. So here she was, sitting on her bunk in the southern building in a cramped little room she now called her own, wishing for some excitement.

As if on cue, a knock came on her door. Sariah's eyes lit up. Maybe she'd have some excitement today, after all.

"Who is it?" she asked.

"It's Ilene, child," a cold voice answered.

Sariah smiled and sat up straight. "Come in!" She

looked around to see if anything in the room was amiss, but of course, it wasn't. She had precious few items in her room other than the bed and a small closet.

Ilene came into the room, looking stoic. She always looked and acted a little regal. Sariah wondered briefly whether or not she was part of some royal family somewhere but decided she most likely was not. No royal family would let their daughter live in a place like this.

"There you are, child," Ilene told her. "I had hoped to find you here this day."

Sariah nodded. "Well, you found me. What's up? Want to know more about Gabe and the Master? Do you need my help with some grand scheme?"

"Something like that," Ilene offered. Her eyes went to the floor, then to the edge of the bed. "Do you mind if I sit? These old joints get tired sometimes."

Sariah scooted over a bit and patted the bunk. "By all means!"

Ilene nodded once and sat down gingerly like she would sink in and never be found if she were to put her full weight down. "Thank you," she replied. She shifted a few times as though she was still uncomfortable.

"So, what is it?" Sariah pressed. This was the first bit of excitement she'd had in two days. She wasn't about to let it pass. "Whatever it is, I'm ready for it!"

The older woman flashed her a tiny smile, then grimaced. "Yes, well, I was hoping you would say that," she replied cryptically. "You are to report to training today."

"Training?" Sariah groaned. Training made her think of the long days she'd spent with Gabe on weapons and magic. A bit of bile pushed up her throat, and she forced it down.

"Yes, child. Training. Blade and magic, both. We must all be at the top of our game if we are to be successful."

The ice lady had a point.

Still, training almost felt like a step down for her. She'd taken on two Dusk Raven leaders and lived, and she'd survived against Gabe as well. Maybe that last one wasn't the best example, but she wasn't in her right mind at the time.

"As in, today?" Sariah asked hesitantly.

"Yes, of course, dearie!" Ilene replied with a chuckle.

It was the first time Sariah had heard her laugh, and somehow the noise didn't sound right coming from her lips. It sounded strained and forced if such a thing were possible with a chuckle.

She bit her lip. "I hate to ask, but is there something else I can do today? I feel like my talents could be better served elsewhere. Like on the front lines."

Ilene looked down at her. "I saw your moves out there in the field the other day, too, if you recall," she admonished. "Your blade work needs some definite improvement. And your magic wasn't any smoother. Anyone with half a brain could have found you. You might have been invisible, but you were still louder than an ape." There was a hint of mirth in the older woman's eyes as she spoke.

Did I really suck that much? Sariah wondered. It was possible, she supposed. It wasn't like anyone had ever really critiqued her magic form.

"Sorry," Sariah offered, hanging her head low. "You're right. When do I start?"

Ilene clapped her hands together. "Excellent. I'll let your arms instructor know to expect you shortly. You'll be late today, but that's of no consequence. You'll do well to report on time from here on out, though. He's a bit of an ass about that."

"Of course, my lady," Sariah replied. She had to force herself not to use the "ice lady" nickname she'd heard several others give her around town.

The older woman got up to leave. She was almost out the door when another thought came to Sariah. "Who is my arms trainer, Ilene? Er, my lady?" she corrected hurriedly.

Ilene turned and smiled at her. In the light and from this lower angle, it looked a little mischievous. "Why Will, of course."

"*Scheisse!*" Sariah swore. She should have guessed as much.

When Sariah reached the training field, she saw Will already grappling with one of the trainees while the rest of them stood at attention.

Scheisse! she swore again in her head. Somehow, she didn't think Will would take kindly to her being late, even with Ilene's blessing. With Ilene not here to defend her, somehow she knew it wouldn't be pretty.

She wasn't sure just what the relationship was between those two. There was obviously some history that neither of them wanted to admit publicly.

As quietly as she could, she snuck up alongside one of

the other trainees standing on the edge of the group and tried to mimic the way he stood. He was standing straight and tall with his hands clasped behind his back and his head straight ahead. It took her a few attempts, but she thought she had it about right.

Not long after, Will pushed the man he had been grappling with away and looked back at the group. A scowl passed over his face as his eyes came into contact with her own.

Here it comes.

"Well, well, well, if it isn't little Sariah," Will sneered. "How nice of you to join us today. Get enough nappy time earlier?"

The implication incensed her, and she wanted to punch him in the face but knew it wouldn't do her any good. He'd probably just dodge her fist anyway.

Instead, she smiled at him. "My apologies, Ilene wanted a word with me. It won't happen again."

She was taking a risk throwing Ilene's name around. She figured it might earn her a few points with her fellow trainees, at least, but wasn't sure what the mention would do to Will. There was still so much she didn't know.

"Of course," Will replied through clenched teeth. It was clear he thought she was showing him up by bringing Ilene into this. That had been her intention, so he wasn't wrong.

Sariah decided not to press the point any further and just kept up the smile.

Will looked a little unnerved by her demeanor, but he kept going. "As I was saying to all of you that bothered to show up on time today," he quipped with another glare in her direction, "If you can find your opponent's weak spot, you'll have the upper hand. And everyone has a weak spot."

His eyes had roved the crowd for most of that last sentence, but as he said the last bit, he looked straight at her and made sure she knew it.

Sariah understood the implication well enough. She'd pressed her luck during the combat trial, and such antics would score her no points during training. She nodded at him briefly, and he seemed satisfied.

"Sir?" one of the recruits piped up. Sariah looked over to see who it was. It was a scrawny kid, barely taller than she was. He had a shock of blond hair, and he looked very uncertain of himself.

"Yes?" Will answered, looking slightly annoyed.

"What if I can't get to their weak spot?"

Sariah wanted to snicker but thought better of it. She could fully believe that a little kid like that wouldn't be able to reach certain spots on a bigger man.

Will huffed. "Try harder. There's always a solution to everything. Just keep looking."

The kid nodded, but he looked like he didn't believe the older man.

"You don't believe me?" Will challenged.

Scrawny Kid shook his head. "No, sir. I mean, yes, sir. Yes, I do."

"Come here, kid," Will commanded, beckoning Scrawny Kid to come forward. "You, too," he said, pointing at another recruit. This one was easily twice Scrawny Kid's size.

"What's your name, kid?" Will asked the scrawny one.

"Albert, sir," he replied in a shaky voice.

"Well, Albert, today I'm going to show you what I mean." He clapped the young man on the back and turned him to face the bigger recruit. "Albert, this is Sean. He'll be your opponent today. I want you to take him down."

Albert gulped nervously but bobbed his head. "Y-yes, sir."

Sean and Albert eyed each other, then Will got out of the way. What happened next could only be described as a massacre. Albert tried his hardest to get under Sean's guard, but the tiny kid barely got a chance to act before Sean side-swiped him with one of his big fists, sending the kid sprawling into the ground.

Will shook his head and went over. "Get up," he demanded. He held out his hand, and the boy took it. Albert dusted himself off.

"Now this time, let me show you what you did wrong. Sean, come over here again."

The older boy walked over. "Now Sean, you move in like you want to hit Albert, just the way you did before, but stop before you hit him."

Sean did as he was bid. He stopped just shy of punching Albert.

"Good," Will said. "Now Albert, I want you to take a good, long look at your friend Sean here. See how he's over-extended himself? He can't possibly balance well like that. There's your chance. You come in low enough with a blow to his leg, and he'll go face-first into the ground instead of you."

Albert eyed Will like he'd grown another head. "Maybe you could, sir, but me?" He pointed at himself and shook his head.

"Nonsense! Try it for yourself."

The kid still looked hesitant, but he did as he was instructed. He crouched down and shoved on Sean's hind leg, but nothing happened.

"See, sir?"

Will rolled his eyes and growled. "No, kid, like this." He spent a few moments adjusting everything about Albert—his stance, the width between his feet, even moved him a few inches to the left. When he was satisfied, he said, "Now kick out as hard as you can. Sean here can take it, can't you Sean?"

The older boy nodded once.

Albert still seemed uncertain, but he did what Will asked and lashed out with a swift kick. Sean's hind leg buckled, and all at once, the big kid came tumbling down. He looked up at Albert, who was now beaming from ear to ear.

"That's my boy!" Will clapped him on the back again, and it almost sent the poor kid flying.

Sariah snickered out loud this time, then clapped her hand over her mouth. It made no difference. Will had picked up on it.

Will was on top of her quicker than she could blink, getting in her face so close she could feel the heat of his breath and smell what he'd had for breakfast. Eggs, apparently. "Something wrong, Sariah?" he demanded. "Did I miss something?"

She stood as straight as she could and shook her head. "No, sir."

Will nodded once and backed away, then turned his back to her. "That's what I thought."

"It's just…" Sariah started, even though she knew it was dangerous to do so. "Do you really think Albert could have done the same thing in the middle of a real battle without you helping him?"

Their trainer turned sharply on his heels and glared at her with a murderous expression. When he spoke, his words were remarkably calm. "With enough training, yes. Yes, he could."

"You're serious, aren't you?" Sariah replied with her head cocked.

"Completely."

She rolled her eyes. "Oh, come on. I mean, with a lot, and I do mean a lot of training, maybe, but I still doubt it."

Will shrugged. "Seemed to work well enough for you. Maybe you'd like to show them how it works, right now? On me?" He had a wicked smile on his face.

The color drained from Sariah's face, and she gulped hard. She knew when she was in over her head. She shook her head slightly. "No, sir."

Will smiled. "Good." He held up a finger. "I have a different test for you. Something more suited to your…talents."

She rolled her eyes, wondering what he could possibly come up with.

When their trainer pulled a few smooth stones out of his pocket and placed them on the ground, it was all she could do not to roll on the floor laughing. "More rocks? Really? I can move rocks easily enough, I assure you," she insisted with a half-giggle.

Will shook his head. "I don't want you to move them,

sweet cheeks. I want you to make them explode using magic."

That stopped Sariah short. She frowned. "Explode them? Is that even possible?"

Will shrugged. "You tell me. It's either that, or we see just how much you've learned about combat over the past two days." He gave her an evil grin.

Sariah let out a sigh and stared at the rocks sitting in the field, staring back at her. She picked one up and ran her finger along the edge, almost expecting to run into a crack like she had with Gabe's prized rocks.

"Ugh," she groaned, then she shook her head to clear it. She really had to stop thinking about Gabe every time she turned around. Inwardly, she wondered if she'd ever stop thinking of him fondly, or at all. Now there was a question that needed an answer. But not now.

Sariah thought about the situation logically. Rocks could be broken with a strong enough tool, so there was no reason one couldn't be shattered with magic if you tried hard enough. Or exploded, rather. He'd been very specific using that term. Simply breaking the rock in two wouldn't suffice. She had to make it blow up like a bomb.

How am I supposed to go about doing that? she wondered. She didn't have much of an answer.

Maybe if I lift the rock high enough, it'll explode when it hits the ground?

She shrugged. She wasn't sure if it would work, but she supposed it was worth a shot. She calmed herself, then made a small lifting motion with her right hand. One of the rocks shot up high into the sky.

A couple of the trainees whistled as they watched the

rock lift into the air, apparently of its own accord. It seemed not all of them had used magic. Or at least, hadn't seen it used like this before.

Sariah let the rock fly upward for another moment, then she let go of the magic, and it came crashing back down to Irth. When it came into contact with the ground, it broke cleanly in two. She frowned. While the whole episode had been impressive in its own right, it hadn't produced the desired effect.

Will huffed. "Give up, then? Can't wait to get your arse handed to you again, maybe?"

She growled at him and held up a hand defensively. The last thing she wanted was to lose this conflict.

"Hang on, I'm not done yet. I've got a few other things to try." She didn't really, but she had to think of something fast.

She furrowed her brow in concentration. Was it even possible to make a rock explode with magic? It had to be. Will's a jerk, but he's at least got to be semi-honorable.

She rubbed her chin. Moving the rock with her mind had caused it to rupture, but not explode. That couldn't be it. Rocks weren't living creatures, so physical magic had to have an answer for her somewhere.

What if she tried to move the rock two different ways at once? Maybe that would do the trick. It was worth a shot.

Just how am I supposed to do that, exactly? Sariah bit her lip. She wasn't sure. It was only one rock. She couldn't move the whole rock two different ways at once. She was right back where she'd started.

Looking up, she saw Will staring at her. His smug face

made it clear he didn't expect her to succeed in this challenge. Somehow, that just made her want it all the more.

She tried to calm her thoughts and focus. There was an answer here, there had to be. All she had to do was find it.

Her gaze returned to the rocks in the middle of the field. There were several. She supposed she could make them fly into each other. Surely, that would cause an explosion.

A brief sigh escaped her lips. That was no different than what she'd done earlier by lifting a rock and letting it drop. That had been pretty much the same thing as smashing them together, and it would end in about the same way, too.

No, she needed something else. Something different. She felt like she was on the right track and just needed to dig a little deeper.

Then it hit her. What if she didn't move the whole rock? What if she willed part of it to move in one direction, and another part the other way? Do that with enough different parts of the rock, and that would look like an explosion for sure.

Her lips curled into a broad smile. She had her answer.

Sariah took a step back and stared at one of the rocks in the field. She imagined it not as one solid piece, but as many tiny granules that made up the whole. Then, she imagined all of those tiny granules flying in different directions at the same time.

As she focused on the rock, she made an outward motion with her hands and poured her energy into the task. At first, nothing happened, but then the rock started to shake violently. It exploded into a thousand tiny pieces, each one flying off in a different direction. The dust cloud it made was so big that people all over Talon's Reach could see it.

Sariah looked at Will. He was coated in rock dust. Somehow, he'd suffered the majority of the blast. She gave him a wry smile.

Will spat out a bit of rock that had flown into his mouth and huffed. "I suppose you think congratulations are in order?" he fired at her. "They're not."

She rolled her eyes. "Oh come on, that was one hell of an explosion!" She looked around. Everyone else in the group was staring at her with their eyes wide and their mouths open. It was obvious she'd beaten their expectations.

Everyone but Will, of course. He was still scowling at her. "Humph," he said at last. "It was passable. Barely. Enough to save your hide for today, at least."

He brushed a little more of the stone off his shoulders. "But tomorrow, I expect better from you. Parlor tricks like that will only get you so far."

She didn't know what it was going to take to impress this guy. It wasn't fair for him to be like this.

"I did what you wanted, didn't I?"

"Humph," he repeated. "It's good enough. For now. Maybe that magic instructor of yours will have more luck making something out of you." He walked over to her and clapped her once on the back. It hurt and made the skin on her shoulder sting a bit. "Good job."

Sariah rubbed the spot where he'd slapped her. She was sure that little jab was going to leave a mark. Still, she had mouthed off a bit, so she supposed she deserved it.

Will turned and looked at all of them. "That's enough for today. You'll give me fifty laps around the field, followed by two hours of sword training with your designated partner before you turn in for the day. Class dismissed."

There were a thousand things on Sariah's mind right then, including where the field he referring to was, and who her partner was supposed to be. She groaned again. These were things she would have known if she'd been on time.

Still, that hadn't been her fault, and Will knew it. He was being unfair to her, and she had half a mind to tell him as much, but then she saw the rest of the recruits running off without her.

Sariah shrieked and ran after them, determined not to be left behind. As she ran, one thought repeated itself over and over in her mind—training was going to suck.

CHAPTER EIGHT

Harvey rubbed at a small spot on his pant leg. It looked like rust, but it was probably just dirt. There was plenty of dirt to be had in the mines. He rubbed and rubbed, but he had precious few resources to work with and didn't want to waste any water, so it was mostly ineffective.

In the end, he figured he'd probably ended up making the spot look worse than it had before.

He let out a deep sigh. Dirty pants seemed like a stupid thing to worry about given his current situation, but it was something he could control, and there weren't many things he could control right now. Besides, it wasn't as though he had a spare pair to change into.

It had been over four weeks they'd been trapped in the mines now, or at least he thought it had been that long. One couldn't tell time all that well trapped in the dark, but he knew he was starting to smell.

Back when he'd been training with Sariah and Gabe, Sariah had been very insistent they bathe regularly. He'd chided her and called it unnecessary and cruel, but now he found himself missing it.

He shook his head to clear the memories. It wouldn't do him any good to dwell on them now. Not down a thousand feet below the surface. Nothing he'd learned would help him and Padron get out of here alive, let alone the rest of the townsfolk that were trapped with them.

Oh sure, there were plenty of magic tricks that might help, like invisibility or mind control, but he'd never had the knack for mental magic. Physical spells were more his thing. Teleportation could come in handy, he supposed, but he couldn't very well teleport half the town out of the mine shaft.

He was determined not to leave the mines without them. They were his people. He needed to protect them.

"It's no use," he said to Padron, shaking his head again. "The pants are ruined."

Padron let out a hearty laugh and clapped him on the back. "Maybe if you ask real nice, the guards will let you borrow theirs." The rearick smiled at him.

Harvey flashed him a dopey grin. "Sure thing. I'm sure they wouldn't mind walking around in their underwear."

They both laughed then, imagining what that would look like—well-armed guards walking around with armored tops and nothing but underwear on the bottom half.

"Ah, lad, yer always good fer a laugh," Padron offered. His friend shook his head then and went back to the mind-less work of digging those blasted amphoralds out of the walls.

Harvey let his eyes wander to the massive cuff around

Padron's ankle. A tear welled up in his eyes as he thought about how painful it must be for him to be chained up like that.

The manacles they were using down here were downright massive and clamped extra tight around the skin. They had to be, lest the miners try to use their pickaxes to break them apart. Nothing short of dynamite would blow one of those chains to pieces, and no one wanted the aftermath of something like that.

Padron had let slip a few days ago that it was really hard to sleep in them, too. Harvey winced at the thought. He could only imagine.

Fortunately, Harvey had so far remained chain-less. He felt both lucky and guilty. It was both a good and a bad thing to be among the lucky few. There were a few like him without chains, though the majority of the workers carried them around all day.

The guards had told him that they needed a few miners who were able to move freely about the area and scout for new veins, which is why he and a few others were still without the chains. They were good scouts. He wasn't as good as Sariah, of course, no one was, but he still knew what to look for.

Every time a vein would run out, he and the other scouts would be sent off to find a new source, then the whole operation would be moved a few painstaking prisoners at a time to the new location. In the time he'd been down here, that had only happened once, and they'd brought enough guards for that move that escaping hadn't been an option.

All in all, it was a pretty miserable setup. Here he was, a

thousand feet below ground, forced to work to further the goals of some evil party while he watched his friends and neighbors grow increasingly weaker and sicker as time went on.

Harvey sighed again. Their outlook was getting grimmer by the day.

"We need to get out of here," Harvey said to Padron.

The rearick shrugged. "Aye, lad, but how? It's not like ye can just walk out the door."

Harvey nodded. "Still, there must be a way. I'm sure of it." His eyes went to the chains again. "Maybe if we try hard enough, we can manage to bust the lock on those things."

Padron shook his head. "Tried that, remember? It didna work so well tha last time." He pointed to a thin gash on his shin.

Harvey looked over the gash and shuddered. It looked slightly infected. Not that the guards would care. If anything, pointing it out would probably only get them into more trouble.

The wound had come from one of their previous escape attempts. Harvey had tried to break the chain lock with a pickaxe, and when that hadn't worked, Padron had used his superior might to try. Only his aim had been a little off, and he'd managed to nick his own leg instead.

After a good bit of swearing, they'd both agreed to stop messing around with the chains.

Harvey wished he'd watched Vincent work his healing spells a little more intently. If he had, maybe he would be able to help his friend now. As it was, there was nothing he could do for him.

He paced the floor. If their situation didn't change, and

soon, he worried Padron would lose the appendage. He couldn't bear to see his friend go through that.

Not to mention, the guards would probably kill the man if it really started to look bad. He couldn't let it come to that.

"We need the key," Harvey offered. "If we could get a hold of a key, we could make quick work of all the chains."

"It's not like they bring tha key down 'ere with 'em, lad," Justine, one of Padron's friends, said in a downtrodden voice. "Not unless they're movin' us, and there's too many of them then."

Harvey looked at the female rearick. She was in chains, too, and her face was even paler than Padron's. He briefly wondered if she was getting sick too, but pushed the thought from his mind. It was of little importance. What was important was breaking free.

"I know that," he spat, continuing to pace the floor. "But someone must have it on them the rest of the time. We just need to find out who."

Justine shrugged. "It won't make no difference, lad. Even if we got our grubby little hands on it, they'd just kill us 'afore we made it out."

"Not if I was able to free us all first. With our superior numbers, we'd…"

"We'd what, lad? Puke on them?" Justine cast her eyes wide to encompass the room. "Look around ya, lad. These folk aren't in tha best 'o health. Ye want to get out 'o here, I suggest ye save yerself."

Harvey scowled and waved his hand at her dismissively, then kept pacing.

How could she just give up like that?

He knew that wasn't fair. Their chances were grim, even without the chains. He looked at his people with fresh eyes. Justine was right. They were slowly dying—all of them.

The sight only incensed him and deepened his desire to act. He needed to rescue them, and he was sure there must be some way to do it. All he needed was a plan.

He looked around the room again for inspiration. It wasn't like they were without tools of defense down here. The guards had taken his sword and Padron's battle-axe ages ago, but pickaxes could make a fine weapon. They weren't as nimble as a sword, perhaps, but they'd get the job done.

Heck, even the manacles around his friends' limbs could be potent as a weapon if it came to it. He just needed to get them off and think of some way to get the drop on the guards and to come at them when they least expected it.

The beginnings of a plan started to form.

Harvey's lips curled into a wry smile. He knew what he had to do, and better yet, he could put the plan into action that very night. The stupid guards would never even know what hit them.

After mealtime, he would have a good twelve hours to test his theory. His stomach growled at him, which likely meant it was soon.

He walked over to where Padron was leaning up against the wall. The rearick was sweating and putting on a good show, but he could tell the man was in pain.

Soon, he thought. I'll have you out of here soon.

"Hey, Padron," he started. "Will the townspeople still listen to you, do you think?"

The rearick wrinkled his nose and glared at him. "Whatcha mean by that, me boy?"

Harvey chuckled slightly. "I've got an idea, but it's going to require quite a bit of coordination. I'll need someone to help set up things here while I'm gone."

A slight chuckle escaped Padron's lips. He looked at the younger man like he'd gone mad. "Pfft. And just where are ya going, lad? It's not like tha mines are that big."

Harvey grinned from ear to ear. "To go get a key, of course." He pulled Padron in close and started whispering in his ear. "This is what I need you to do…"

***

Taking a deep breath, Harvey worked to calm his nerves. He ran a hand through his hair, and his fingers were shaking.

And this is the easy part, he thought wryly.

That wasn't entirely accurate. Escaping the mine was the easy part since he could just teleport outside the door. He had no idea what was waiting for him on the other side, though. Heck, he was only mildly certain it was night time. If he appeared in the wrong spot, his little stealth mission would be over before it even started.

He took another deep breath to calm himself and wiped a bead of sweat from his brow.

"Now or never," he told himself. He rubbed his face once, then steadied his hands and concentrated on the other side of the door.

An instant later, he was through. He immediately ducked low and took a look around. He was right next to a minecart, and he used it for cover while he scouted the area. Fortunately, no one seemed to have noticed him.

In fact, there was only one guard in the front of the mine, and he looked like he was either snoring or staring off into space. It was hard to tell from Harvey's angle, only that the man wasn't paying him any attention.

The mine entryway was lit up by several torches, making it hard to gauge if it was day or night. Harvey focused on the sky outside the entrance. A thick blanket of stars greeted his eyes, and he breathed a slight sigh of relief. It was indeed nighttime, and better yet, a mere sliver of the moon was out, which meant there would be even less light to spot him by.

That was a good thing because he'd never been all that great at mental magic. Invisibility was beyond his grasp. He'd have to settle for moving slow and quiet instead.

He crept from behind his hiding spot and inched closer to the guard. The man was motionless and oblivious to his movements. A few more steps closer, and he was able to confirm his suspicion that the man was fast asleep and snoring up a storm.

Emboldened by the sleeping guard, Harvey sprinted past and into the relative safety of the darkness beyond the mine entrance.

Phase one complete. He breathed another sigh of relief.

He took a look around to get his bearings. He used to know the area like the back of his hand, but much had changed. There were new buildings, and guard towers set up at intervals, and roaming guard patrols that crossed the main thoroughfare every few minutes.

The mine foreman seemed to be taking no chances these days. Not that Harvey could blame the guy. If the situation were reversed, he'd probably do the same thing.

Harvey crouched behind a low wall in full view of the walkway and studied the guard patterns for several minutes. He couldn't afford to slip up here even a little bit.

If worse came to worst, he could probably use his magic to get out of a scuffle, but then an alarm would be raised and his mission would be for naught. It was imperative that he not get caught.

He watched two guards walk past his spot and head down the walkway toward the exit of the mine complex. Then he counted to twenty and stuck his head over the wall.

The guards were nowhere to be seen. Harvey wiped his forehead again, then he got moving. He figured he had about five minutes to make it to another safe spot before the next round of patrols.

His progress was painfully slow as he had to stop regularly when he heard one of the guards up ahead make a weird noise, or he had to retake his bearings. It pained him to move so slowly through an open area. Finally, he managed to find his way into another alcove where he could breathe easily for a couple of minutes.

Harvey stared down the path that went past his location. At the end of it stood a massive building, undoubtedly a barracks of some sort. There were probably keys aplenty inside, but also soldiers. He couldn't risk going in there.

A little off to the side, down a branching path, was a

much smaller building. It looked relatively nondescript, but the door was in much better shape than any of the surrounding ones.

His lips curled into a smile. That was his target—the foreman's residence.

Just then, another guard patrol came walking by, and he had to dodge back into the shadows of the alcove to avoid being seen.

As the guards walked past his position, Harvey's heart beat so fast he could hear it in his ears. He was half-shocked that the guards didn't pick up on it as well.

The two guards stopped a few feet in front of him. One of them started looking around.

A chill ran down Harvey's spine, and his heart practically stopped. Had they seen me? he wondered.

"Long night," the one on the left said.

"Aye," the other guard said with a nod. "Can you believe Freddie? Snoring away so loud he could practically wake the dead!"

Left Guard snorted. "He better not let the foreman catch him is all I can say."

Right Guard chuckled. "That fatso's probably asleep 'imself, assuming his mistress is done with him by now."

Left Guard clapped Right Guard on the back. "Aye, you've got a point. They're quite the pair those two. Both snorin' away while us little folk do all the hard work."

Right Guard shrugged. "Ain't nothin' to it. That's just the breaks." Right Guard shivered slightly and pulled on his tunic. "Come, let's finish our shift so we can get some shut-eye of our own."

Left Guard nodded and snorted again. "How can you be

cold in this heat?" He smacked Right Guard lightly on the back of the head. "Fine, let's get going."

Harvey heard a few more chuckles and the sound of footsteps heading away from him. He waited for what felt like a half an hour before he moved again, then he finally ducked his head out from his hiding spot.

He was in the clear.

This time, he hurried as fast as he dared toward the building with the new door. He hadn't been tracking the seconds that well, and he wasn't sure how long it would be until the next set of guards.

He made it to the door with no further surprises. Trying the handle, he was surprised to find it unlocked.

Finally, he had a spot of luck.

Moving slowly to keep the noise to a minimum, he turned the handle and let the door swing open. It creaked a little, but thanks to its newness opened quite easily.

Harvey stepped halfway into the room and looked around. Inside was dark, and there was an overturned piece of furniture near the entryway. Most importantly, there was no sign of anyone moving.

He crept the rest of the way into the room and shut the door softly behind him, then gave his eyes a few minutes to adjust to the inky darkness of the interior.

It didn't take him too long.

He crept over to the overturned chair and used it for cover while he took in the rest of the room. It was empty except for a couch in one corner and a chamber pot that looked to be recently used in the other. At the far end of the room stood another half-open door.

Harvey wrinkled his nose a bit as the smell from the

chamber pot wafted across his nostrils. He avoided making any noise and moved over toward the door, pushing it open.

With all the courage he could muster, he surveyed the new room. Sure enough, the mine foreman Jeffrey was lying on a bed in the middle of the room, snoring away softly. Some girl was in bed next to him, wearing very little and snoring as well.

It didn't take a vivid imagination to figure out what they'd gotten up to.

As for his goal, he saw it hanging, not five feet from the bed. On the wall hung a small keyring with a thick, iron key on it. That must be what he was looking for. It made sense the foreman would keep it on or near his person. He didn't seem to be the most trusting type. He'd want to keep it close.

Harvey slunk over and carefully removed the keyring from the wall. It made a slight creaking sound as the metal of the keyring grated against the metal hook, then it was free. He looked over at the foreman and his girl to see if they had heard him. Fortunately, they had not.

Standing there in the low light, Harvey caught a glimpse of something weird on Jeffrey's palm. He took a step closer and squinted to examine it. There on the foreman's right palm, plain as day, was a small raven tattoo.

Blood rushed to Harvey's head and anger filled him. The foreman was a Dusk Raven. He contemplated killing the man right then and there in his sleep but thought better of it. That would definitely be noticed.

Much as he hated to admit it, the foreman's death would have to wait for another day. Instead, he took a few steps toward the door to leave the room. The thought of killing him kept coming back, but he pushed it down each time, denying the urge.

When he was about halfway out of the room, a different thought came to him, and he frowned.

Surely the foreman would notice the key was gone.

That would ruin the element of surprise, and Harvey's plan depended on it. He had to think of something. There was always illusion magic, but he wasn't any good at it. Besides, he wasn't sure if he could keep up the illusion if he wasn't in the vicinity. He needed something else.

Thinking fast, he spotted a spare dagger on the floor. Once again, the thought of killing the foreman came to mind. It would be so easy to take that dagger and slit his throat. But now was not the time.

Still, the blade could be of use. Its color was pretty close to the color of the iron key. It was a longshot, but it was better than nothing.

Harvey's fingers twitched a few times, and the metal in the dagger warped until it formed a neat circle with a small iron piece jutting out of one side.

He held his creation up next to the actual key and admired his handiwork. All in all, they looked pretty similar. A careful inspection would reveal the warped dagger was a fake, but maybe it would buy him enough time to set his plan into motion.

Harvey walked back to the hook for the keyring. As he did so, he stepped on a loose floorboard and made an awful racket. Jeffrey's snoring stopped.

He froze in place and waited several moments. Soon, Jeffrey started snoring again. Harvey let out a quiet sigh of relief and crossed the rest of the room in as few steps as possible. He hung up the fake key and then hightailed it back to the entrance of the building.

Sticking his head out of the doorway, he looked around for guards. There weren't any at the moment, but he hadn't been keeping track of time in the foreman's house, so that wasn't much of a consolation.

A moment later, he heard the sound of feet shuffling and a moan from within the house. It seemed that Jeffrey or his mistress were waking at last.

Harvey gulped down the knot of fear forming in his chest and decided to act fast. Teleporting out of here was risky, but far less so than getting caught. He'd just have to hope for the best.

As he prepared his spell, he wondered if Padron had been successful in relaying his plan to the other prisoners. Only time would tell. Soon enough, they'd all be free or dead. That is if he got out of there in one piece.

"Hey!" a voice said from behind him. "Who's there?"

Time's up, Harvey thought.

He gripped his newfound key tightly and focused on the mine's interior. A moment later, he disappeared into the night.

CHAPTER NINE

"Take that!" Sariah hissed. A white-hot jet of flame shot forth from her fingers, incinerating the nearby woodpile. The flames greedily licked at the dry wood, eating it up and lighting up the pre-dawn sky. Her eyes gleamed in the firelight.

"Excellent," a voice from behind her said.

She turned to look at Noah, her magic teacher. He had a broad grin on his face.

"Thank you," she replied shrugging. "At least I'm improving."

Noah nodded. "Indeed. Now finish the sequence."

Sariah flashed him a grin and returned her attention to the woodpile. She made a wiggling motion with her fingers, and a sheet of ice coated the wood, dousing the flames. The training arena went dark, and it took her a second to regain her focus.

Next, she turned her hand palm up and lifted it. The wood planks lifted with her movement, rising high into the sky. She held them there for a moment, then both her hand and the wood came crashing down in unison.

With an audible grunt, she lifted both hands and brought them together. At the same time, a layer of fresh dirt rose up and covered the woodpile. Before long, it was impossible to tell the wood had ever been there.

She panted a few times and wiped a bead of sweat from her brow. "It's done." She turned to face Noah, who nodded again.

"Great work, Sariah. I feel like you're really getting the hang of handling each element on its own," he told her.

She beamed at him. This had been her life for the past three weeks now. Waking up well before dawn to train in magic with Noah, then a few hours of weapons training with Will, followed by group training with the other recruits. Rinse and repeat.

This was her favorite part of the day. Noah taught her magic in ways that were easy for her to understand, and it felt as though he really liked and appreciated her.

He was night and day from Will.

A shudder ran down her spine. She'd have to face him in battle in an hour or so, and she didn't feel ready.

"Is something bothering you, Sariah?" her teacher asked.

She bit her lip and looked up at him. "No, sir." She gave him a wry grin. "We're good. What's the next lesson?"

Noah rubbed his chin for a moment. "Now Sariah, we're not going to get anywhere long as you stay closed off." He reached over and placed a hand gently on her shoulder. "I can tell something's bothering you. If your mind's not in it, you're not going to excel."

Sariah groaned. He sounded just like Will at that moment. Thinking about her next training session made her stomach churn, and she turned away.

"It's nothing," she insisted.

Her instructor tsked. "You're thinking about Will's training again, aren't you?"

She spun around, eyes wide and mouth agape. "How did you know?"

"I'm not an idiot. I know you two don't get along well."

Her cheeks burned. "Is it that obvious?"

Noah let out a deep laugh. "Is the sky blue?" He shook his head. "Look, what if I were to tell you that physical magic can do more than control the elements around you? What if I were to tell you that it could help you with your sword work, too?"

Sariah's eyes almost popped out of her skull. "What do you mean?"

"Heh. I knew that would get your attention." He paused for a moment, head bowed, then he looked into her eyes. "Physical magic can control your body as easily as it can control flames. Make you faster. Stronger. React better. I can show you how."

A broad grin formed on Sariah's lips. This could be just what she needed to finally prove to Will that she was good enough.

"Let's do it."

"Hiya!" Sariah growled as she pushed her blade forward. She lashed out with all the might and speed she could muster, but Will still managed to parry her attack with ease.

She furrowed her brow and scowled at him. How was he so good?

"Your front foot is too far forward," he chided her. "I could lop it off with ease from this angle."

Sariah huffed, but she adjusted her position. Will was right. She'd left herself exposed. Will might hate her, but his critiques on her form were always on point, and she was getting better.

Gabe never taught me like this, she mused.

Her stomach lurched at the thought of Gabe, and she felt a strange tingling in her chest. She supposed it could be heartache. Gabe had been a big part of her life. He'd been her first real mentor, her first kiss. She'd always remember that fondly.

With her mind focused on Gabe, she didn't see Will's practice blade come at her, and it rapped her on the forehead.

"Ow!" Sariah groaned, rubbing the spot. She was pretty sure it was going to leave a nasty bruise.

"Your fault," Will quipped. "You need to stay focused, air brain."

"Ugh." She rolled her eyes, but inwardly, she knew Will was right. Worse, he was always right. No matter what the topic was, he always seemed to know the answer to everything.

It was annoying and exhausting. But what could she do? He was her teacher.

"If you lose focus during a real combat situation, you're dead," Will continued. "You need to keep your mind centered on the matter at hand. Ruminating on the past can wait for later. Rule one, remember?"

"Yes sir," she replied in a disgusted tone. Him and his stupid rules. He had one for everything. Rule one was to always keep your mind in the present. Which, she had to admit, was a good rule. Even if it did come from him.

A smile crept across Will's lips. "Very good. Now try that last move again. This time, don't overextend your foot. Remember to keep your hand at chest level so you can control the blade better."

Sariah nodded and gripped her blade tight, pushing all thoughts of Gabe and their ill-fated relationship behind her. Then she made the slight adjustment and lunged forward.

Once again, Will blocked the blow with ease.

"Grr!" Sariah growled. She mentally reprimanded herself and shook her head.

Don't get angry, get better she heard in her head. It was another of Will's stupid rules. Rule twelve, she thought. She even said it in his mocking voice.

"Much better. A worse opponent would have been skewered there," Will said, looking smug. "Of course, I'm no weakling. Try again. This time remember to follow the tip of your sword with your eyes and look at where you want it to go, not where it is. The sword is an extension of your arm. It goes where you tell it to."

Sariah swung her blade again, swinging it a tiny bit higher this time. Will deflected the blow like he wasn't even trying.

She wiped a bead of sweat from her brow and noted that while she was working hard and sweating profusely,

Will hadn't even broken a sweat. The thought angered her further.

"Try again," Will insisted.

Grunting, she complied. She swung her blade again. And again. And again. No matter how she switched things up—moving higher or lower, faster, slower, or leading with her off-hand—nothing made a difference. All her offensive maneuvers were met with his stoic stance and a quick deflection.

"Not bad," Will told her. "But your legs were still too far apart on those last few swipes. You need to watch your feet lest your opponent cut them off and take that worry away for you."

Sariah groaned, but he was right. If she was honest, she could tell the difference between her first few strikes and the last. Her legs ached a little in response, and she frowned at them.

She wished someone else was there with her so she could have a break, but they were training alone. The rest of the group wasn't due for another hour or so.

They trained with various weapons during solo time. Mostly sword work, though they also practiced with throwing daggers, spears, and hand axes. Will had insisted that he was pulling her aside for these sessions because she was "ahead of the pack," and he wanted to help her in ways he couldn't in a group training session.

She figured it was just extra punishment because he didn't like her. It wasn't like he was ever nice to her during any of the training sessions, group or no. He was always insulting her and insisting she wasn't "living up to her potential."

It was like Gabe's training, but a hundred times worse, and so much harder.

Still, she could only complain so much. She had learned a lot from him, and her skill was definitely improving. It didn't always feel like it since he continued to beat her easily. Even on her best day, and today was not her best day.

Another rap from Will's practice blade came, striking her in the arm.

Sariah gasped and almost let her own blade drop, then gave Will a dirty look.

"What was that for?"

He returned her icy gaze stare for stare. "I told you, rule one. Every time you lose focus, you're going to earn a new bruise."

"Ugh," she whined. As annoying as it was to admit it, she had wandered off mentally again.

"Now try again. Faster this time and point the blade down a bit more on the follow-up."

Try again, she mimicked in a mocking tone. Like she hadn't been trying before.

Sariah shook her head and calmed herself. She could do this. She could get past his guard. She changed up the grip on her blade and started in with a high swing, then abruptly turned the blade downward, aiming toward Will's middle. He managed to deflect this blow as well, but he had to move back a little bit to do it in time.

Her lips curled upward into a smile. She was getting closer. Her mild success emboldened her, so she followed that strike up with a quick succession of blows meant to force Will further back.

Will parried those as well, of course, but only barely, and he was forced backward as she'd hoped.

She kept up the assault, trying to force Will toward a nearby wall so he'd have less room to maneuver. She knew she couldn't beat him dead-on in the middle of the field, but maybe if she could hamper him in some fashion, she'd succeed at last.

Out of the corner of her eye, she caught a glimpse of a small girl watching the two of them from the edge of the courtyard. She couldn't have been more than seven or eight. The girl had a frown on her face like she was upset about something.

What's she doing out here at this hour of the morning? she wondered. She didn't allow herself to think about it for long, lest she failed in her quest.

Returning her focus to the task at hand, she lunged forward with her blade, pushing Will closer to the wall. They were maybe five feet from it now. A few more well-timed pushes, and he'd be backed up against it.

Will seemed to guess her motives, for the next time she lunged forward, he dodged to the left instead of moving backward. He came forward then and rapped her across the back with his practice blade.

Sariah's back screamed out in pain and she almost dropped to the ground, but she remained firm. She stood up straight and glared at Will, then advanced on him again.

The little girl on the sidelines let out a slight gasp, and Sariah let herself look at the young maiden for just a moment. Her frown was replaced by a grimace and she was biting her lower lip.

Was that little girl rooting for her? Lots of little girls

had rooted for her in her skirmishes back at home. They had looked up to her because she could take care of herself, and most of them couldn't.

Her attention focused on the girl for another half-second, then snapped back to the fight just in time to see Will's blade bearing down on her once again. She brought her own weapon up and managed to stop his sword from earning her another bruise.

Emboldened by blocking the attack and by the little girl's rapt attention, Sariah pressed her attack even harder. No longer worried about backing Will into a corner, she came at him instead with a rapid series of blows meant to knock him to the ground.

Her eyes turned coal black as she recalled her training from this morning. She channeled magic into her sword arm and made another strike. Her blade danced through the air and made loud, whooshing noises as it moved.

She gasped a little at just how much faster she was able to move but didn't let it distract her. Instead, she pressed the attack. Will was still parrying her blows, but the blocks were coming slower and with less enthusiasm. Or maybe she was just that much faster. Either way, she was wearing him down.

With a wry smile on her lips, Sariah took one more massive lunge forward, trying to come under Will's guard to slice at his midsection.

Success! She heard a loud thud as her practice blade smacked him squarely in the abdomen and sent Will stumbling backward.

The big man managed to stay upright and kept a hold of his blade, but his face looked surprised.

Sariah raised her blade to strike again, but Will held his hand up in surrender.

"Hold," he commanded. His tone was firm, but not harsh.

She nodded at him once and lowered her practice blade. She spared a glance for the little girl on the sidelines and saw that she was now smiling. Sariah had been right. The girl had been rooting for her. She was suddenly glad that she'd lived up to her expectations.

"I got you," Sariah said to Will unapologetically. "I win." She flashed him a giant smile and took a little bow.

Will glared at her for a moment, then his face softened a little bit. "That was...adequate," he offered. "For today, at least."

Sariah balked. "Adequate? That was pretty damn amazing!"

"Humph," Will replied. "I went easy on you. If I had used magic to enhance my performance, too, you wouldn't have stood a chance. It was a passable attempt, but barely."

"Passable?" Blood rushed to her cheeks, and she felt her face grow hot. "That was some excellent swordsmanship! Admit it, I beat you fair and square."

"Don't get cocky on me now," Will insisted. "You won for today, but only because I let you. Don't you ever mistake ease for skill, or you won't last one minute on the battlefield."

His words were making her skin crawl, and she was getting more upset by the moment. She'd already seen success on the battlefield before this. She knew how to handle herself. Heck, she'd beat him twice now.

"I think you're just jealous," she quipped, placing her hands on her hips.

"Jealous?" Now his eyes widened, and his expression became furious. "Pfft. There's not a jealous bone in my body!"

"Then why are you so hard on me?" Sariah spurted out. "You put me through the most insane training regimens for hours on end, and when I pass your tests, you seem more pissed off than impressed! What gives?"

She was taking a big risk laying it out on the line, but she was fed up with his treatment of her. He'd behaved poorly from the moment they'd met, even calling her a liar in front of everyone. Who was he to judge her past?

Will opened his mouth wide and wagged a finger like he was going to yell at her, then he stopped and lowered his hand to his side. His face softened and his eyes took on a kind look, one she hadn't seen before.

"Is that what you really think?" he asked.

Sariah nodded. "It's common knowledge you don't like me. Everyone knows it."

He shook his head and let out a big breath. Sariah noted he looked a lot like Gabe used to when he was about to apologize. Another twinge of pain rocked her chest. She pushed thoughts of him far away and looked at Will instead.

"It's not like that," Will started. "Well, not exactly. It's no secret I don't believe that trumped-up story of yours. A girl like you, with your skill level beating two Dusk Raven masters?" He shook his head. "Impossible."

Sariah opened her mouth to argue, but Will raised a hand to shush her. "Don't go arguing with me right now, I don't want to hear it. If you really did accomplish such things, I'm sure you'll be a great asset in the battles to come. But that's a big if."

Part of her wanted to shout at him or punch him in the gut and walk away, but instead she gulped down her feelings. "Fair enough. That still doesn't explain your treatment of me, though. Why are you putting me through the wringer? What did I do to you? Is it because I beat you that first time?"

"Humph." Will crossed his arms and shook his head. "That only happened because you cheated."

"Then it was because I beat you! I knew it!"

Will's jaw dropped, and he waved his arms. "Now wait for just a second! That has nothing to do with it!"

Sariah crossed her own arms and gave him a smug smile. "Yeah? What is it, then?" She lifted one hand to her hair and bounced it. "Am I too pretty for you?" she asked in a demure tone.

Will looked incredulous. His cheeks flushed. "That's not it, either!"

It was clear Sariah had gotten under his skin with that one. She chuckled a little on the inside.

"You don't get it, do you?" Will told her. "All this stuff, magic, swordplay, it comes easy to you, no?"

Sariah thought for a moment and rubbed her chin, then nodded. "I guess so. I've never really thought about it before."

"Heh. Somehow I'm not surprised," Will snapped. "Look, these talents don't come easy to everyone. You think Albert or Sean could take you, even after a month of training?"

Sariah thought about it for a moment before answering. She'd been in several training sessions with the two men, both of the magic and sword swinging varieties. Both of them had some talent, for sure, but she had to admit they were no match for her in either field.

"You're saying I'm a natural at this stuff?" Sariah asked.

"You could say that. At the very least, you're no run of the mill soldier, that's for sure."

Sariah was taken aback. Will was complimenting her on her abilities. It was a first for him, and she had to admit she kind of liked it. After weeks of abuse, it felt nice to hear something positive, even if it had been done under duress.

"Well...thank you, I guess," she offered.

"Humph," he replied. "Well, don't let it go to your head. The last thing I need is you dying from overconfidence."

She couldn't stop herself and burst out laughing.

Will glared at her until she stopped. "Did I say something funny to you? Do you take life that glibly?"

Sariah shook her head vehemently. "No. I mean, no, sir, I don't."

He eyed her critically, and she felt a shiver run up her spine as he did so. He turned slightly to the side and cocked his head in her direction. "Good. You'd do well to remember that, recruit."

She nodded. "Yes, sir." She gave him a fake salute and flashed him another grin.

Will seemed to grin back at her for just a second, then it was gone, replaced with his usual serious frown. "Look, what I'm trying to say is that you're good at this stuff. You could do just about anything you wanted to. I'm not sure there are limits for people like you. Especially with magic."

"But, everyone has limits to their abilities, right?" Sariah responded. "I mean, use too much magic, and you'll...you know, explode and stuff, right?"

Will side-eyed her. "Is that what your former teacher told you?" He shook his head. "No wonder you're such a hard student."

"It's true, right?" she insisted. "Come on, it has to be true."

Will huffed again. "Why, because your sorta-boyfriend Gabriel said so?" He rolled his eyes. "And everything he told you was on the up and up, right?"

Sariah opened her mouth to reply but stopped short when she had nothing to say to that. Had Gabe been lying to her about something as basic as that, too?

There was no way to be sure. Maybe he'd believed it, or perhaps he'd been trying to limit her to make sure she never grew stronger than him. Both were believable scenarios.

"I guess you have a point there," Sariah said at last.

Will walked over and placed a big hand gently on her shoulder. His touch was somehow warm and comforting, which she hadn't expected given his usually gruff demeanor. "Look, four weeks ago, I would have told you it was impossible to make a rock explode with your mind. But you managed to make it happen. So who knows what's really possible if you set your mind to it?"

Sariah nodded once without really thinking. Then, her eyes went wide and she pushed Will away. "Wait a second," she said in an accusatory tone. "You mean you didn't think I could explode the rock, but you made me do it anyway?"

Will replied with a sheepish grin and a shrug of his shoulders, then threw his hands up in the air.

She shoved him again, harder this time. "You idiot! Why'd you give me the task if you didn't think I could complete it?"

He sighed once and pulled on his face. "I was trying to get back at you for that stunt you pulled during the trial, okay? You made a fool out of me in front of half the town. I wanted to get back at you in front of the recruits!"

Sariah thought about his answer. She supposed it made sense. It was only fair, given the circumstances.

"Yeah, well, I sure showed you, didn't I?" she replied with a wry smile.

He nodded. "Yeah, you sure did. See what I mean? Who knows what your limits would be if you never knew you had any? You believed you could explode that rock, so you did. With confidence like that, anything could be possible."

Sariah put a finger to her lips, thinking about the possibilities.

What could I do, if only I let myself do it? She didn't have an answer right then, but it was a nice question to ponder.

Will cleared his throat, and she returned her attention to the big man. "Anyway, it'll be time for the other recruits to join us soon. Do you want to get in another half hour of weapons training before they come?" He paused for a second and held a finger up. "This time, we'll both use magic."

A broad smile crept across her lips. "Do I ever!"

He grinned back at her. "I was hoping you'd say that." He walked over to the rack of practice weapons and pulled out a dagger-shaped weapon. He held it in his off-hand and picked up his practice sword in his main hand. "Feel free to use whatever weapons you like this time. No restrictions."

Sariah looked over at the rack, then at the sword she'd let drop to her feet. She picked it up and fingered it gingerly. "I think I'll stick to just this one," she told him. "It's kind of grown on me."

Will raised his eyebrows and cocked his head to the side. "Going against a two-blade wielder with only one of your own? How confident of you." His smile grew broader. "Something I'll have to correct."

Sariah narrowed her eyes and gave him an icy stare. "Oh, I'm not worried one bit."

Her eyes darted around, looking for the little girl who had been silently cheering her on earlier. She was eager to show the young maiden what a real fight looked like. Alas, she seemed to have scurried back to wherever she belonged. Perhaps her parent had come and collected her when Sariah had been talking with Will.

She returned her attention to her opponent, who was staring at her menacingly with an odd look in his eyes that spoke of desire. For the coming battle, she thought. He was a tad bloodthirsty.

"Ready?" Will asked her. He remained perfectly still while he spoke, like a big hulking tower looking down on her.

Sariah nodded at him. "Ready as I'll ever be," she countered.

His lips curled upwards into an evil grin and then he was on her, rushing forward with both blades held in front, each aiming for a different spot on her body.

Sariah pulled up her own blade to block the first lunge and took a half step back to dodge out of the way of the second, smaller blade. She looked into Will's eyes and pushed forward with her sword arm to force him backward and give her some space to retaliate.

This is going to be harder than I thought, she mused. But she didn't mind that one bit.

CHAPTER TEN

Gabriel had a permanent scowl on his face. He was wroth with how events had turned out, and he swore the next person who so much as looked at him wrong was going to pay for it with their life.

He was still furious the stupid dress merchant Valerie had managed to elude his grasp back in Stratton. She hadn't been at the stall as he'd thought she would be, and nearly half the marketplace had paid for it.

For a moment, he felt a twinge of guilt for how that had turned out, but only a twinge, and then it was gone. It was their own stupid fault for not allowing him the vengeance he so richly deserved.

Afterward, he'd scoured nearly every nook and cranny of Stratton, seeking her hiding place, but had come up empty. Even Evelyn, the innkeeper at The Dragonfly that knew all the goings-on in the underworld, had come up empty in the search.

The last anyone had heard, the woman known as Valerie had simply vanished several days earlier without a trace, leaving her bustling clothing business to rot. One day she'd been hawking her wares, and the next, she was gone with nothing to show for it. No one knew where or how she'd left the city. Which was odd, considering it had only one main gate and no side entrances to speak of.

He shook his head, but his thoughts kept returning to the stupid dress merchant. His eyes smoldered, and his blood practically boiled at the thought of her. She would pay, one way or another. He would make sure of it. Then he could finally repair things between him and Sariah.

It was the only shot he had left, the only path forward that even made sense to him anymore. Sariah would see his side of things. She just had to. But first, he had to put an end to the person who had driven the wedge between them in the first place.

The fact he was going to make that ending as painful as humanly possible was just icing on the cake.

Which was why he was here, walking around in the middle of nowhere a hundred or more miles south of Chatwick, in a dingy town he'd only heard of a few times prior.

The town of Esterlily. It was nowhere near as big or grand as Stratton, though it was nestled close to the shore of the ocean. From where he was perched outside the town, he could see several massive ships in the distance, each filled with goods of one kind or another.

Looking around, he could understand why a man like Zachariah would like it here. The presence of ships and water meant he could travel a great many other places without resorting to magic. Unlike Gabe, Zachariah only used magic when he had no other choice, like traveling north for councils with the Master.

Plus, sailors made excellent spies. Few people suspected them of anything untoward, so they were in prime positions to listen in on their guests' lives.

Zachariah's spy network had brought Gabe to this place today. If anyone were to have an idea about where Valerie had gotten off to, it would be Zachariah's spies. They had to know something. He was sure of it.

Gabe kept walking down the main road that led into town. It was broad daylight, and he made no attempt to hide his appearance or purpose.

In fact, it might be better if one of Zachariah's spies caught wind of him early. It'd save him the trouble of announcing himself.

Out of the corner of his eye, Gabe caught sight of a small man scurrying for the main gate. Undoubtedly it was one of those spies, gone to inform his master.

Gabe huffed. It looked like he'd been right, after all.

A few minutes later, he spotted the city's main gate. It was a broad stone arch, adorned with flowers and streamers running along it. The sight was much too bright and cheery for his tastes, but then it wasn't his home.

Standing in contrast to the bright and cheery entrance was a tall, muscular man blocking the entryway. He was wearing leather armor and brandishing a massive spear in one hand. He was flanked by two equally large men.

Gabe smiled at the man, whose frown only deepened in response.

"Ho, there," Gabe called out, holding his hands out in front of him in a sign of friendship.

Zachariah scowled at him. "Well met, Gabriel," he said slowly through clenched teeth. It was obvious the big man didn't mean it.

Gabe saw Zachariah's hand tighten on the shaft of his spear. He held his hands up higher in response. "Rest easy, friend. I am not here to challenge you today."

Zachariah's eyes trailed up and down his body. The man huffed. "Then what do you come seeking today, friend?" he retorted. The last word he practically spat out in disgust.

Gabe smiled bigger. "Worry not, I'm only here for information. I hear you're good at that sort of thing."

Zachariah's grip on his spear loosened just a little bit, and the man's face softened. Gabe snorted in disgust at how easily the man let his guard down. If he had done the same, he'd surely be dead by now. To each their own, he supposed.

"Fine, but it'll cost you. Information isn't free," the other man replied.

Gabe let out a slight chuckle. "Okay. Name your price."

"How am I supposed to know the price when I don't know what you seek?"

Gabe rubbed his chin thoughtfully. That was fair. Still, he didn't want to spill everything. Not out in the open in front of dozens of other spies. What if word got out about his little quest? Some might think his need for vengeance was a weakness they could exploit.

In the end, he settled on a vague explanation. "I'm looking for someone. An elderly woman of some...import."

Zachariah's brow raised just a fraction. "That is not a

lot to go on, friend." Again, he spat the last word more than spoke it.

Gabe shrugged. "It's all I'm willing to divulge in the open. What's your price for someone's whereabouts? I'm sure I can double your standard rate."

The big man rubbed his chin. "Hmm, I bet you could. Still, I have no desire for your possessions. I have plenty enough of my own." He waved his hand about to encompass the town as he spoke in a show of superiority.

Gabe rolled his eyes. "Oh, come on, man, get on with it. Just name your price, already."

Zachariah thrust the butt of his spear into the ground and scowled. "I will not have you lay waste to my traditions on my own soil!" he declared.

Gabe threw up his hands in defeat, then lowered them. He gave a short bow. "Sorry, I'm just in a bit of a hurry. You understand."

Zachariah nodded. "That I do." He rubbed his face with his free hand. "Fine, my price is thus. I want a favor from you."

"A favor?" Gabe rocked back on his heels. His eyes narrowed. "What kind of favor?"

"Whatever I want. I shall call on you at a future date, and you will do what I ask of you then. Do we have a deal?"

Gabe thought for a moment. Zachariah tapped his foot impatiently like he didn't have all day to worry about this. Should I accept? he wondered. He supposed it would be fine. He had no intention of paying the debt anyway. He'd sooner kill the man.

With that decided, Gabe relented. He nodded once.

"Deal. Now can we go someplace a little more private to discuss this?"

The big man smiled, revealing a few missing teeth. "Of course."

Zachariah motioned for Gabriel to enter a nondescript building slightly off of the main pathway of Esterlily. He had to duck his head a bit, but he went inside. Zachariah followed.

Gabe wondered briefly why the man would choose a house where he had to duck his head to get in, then chuckled softly. At his height, the man likely didn't have a choice. He stood a half a hand taller than Gabe, and Gabe wasn't exactly short.

Zachariah shut the door behind them and motioned for Gabe to take a seat at a table that stood in the exact center of the room.

"Any seat in particular?" Gabe asked. The big man shook his head.

Gabe shrugged and picked a particularly ornate chair near the head of the table. He figured it probably belonged to his host, which was why he chose it. He hoped it would help get under the man's skin.

Zachariah, for his part, seemed completely unfazed. He took a rather plain-looking chair about halfway up the table and sat down. The chair creaked in protest, but it held together just fine.

So," Gabe started. "About that favor. What did you have in mind?"

Zachariah waved one of his hands dismissively. "Don't worry about that. I'll call on you when I have a need." The big man leaned forward and placed his elbows on the table. He steepled his hands together. "I'm more concerned right now with your person of interest. Tell me everything you can about them. Leave no detail out."

Gabe leaned back in his chair. "There's not a lot to know, unfortunately."

The big man raised an eyebrow. "Surely, there must be something. You wouldn't have come all the way down here without something concrete."

Gabe sighed. "True. She goes by the name of Valerie. She's an elderly lady that frequents the town of Stratton. She sells dresses and clothes there, outside of Dusk Raven influence."

He had been hoping to get a reaction out of his host by emphasizing that last part, but it was ineffective. Zachariah remained stiff.

"Go on," the big man insisted after a moment's pause.

"That's it, really. That's all I know. She disappeared a week or two ago, and no one's seen hide nor hair of her since. It's like she vanished in a puff of smoke." He conveniently left out what he'd done when he'd learned that little detail—no sense in scaring the help.

Zachariah lowered his arms and leaned back a little. He narrowed his eyes and was lost in thought for several moments. "That's not a lot to go on," he uttered at last.

Gabe shrugged. "Maybe not, but it's all I've got." He side-eyed his host. "Besides, I know you've worked with less before. At least I have the name right."

The big man returned his gaze to Gabriel. "That is true.

Still, the less information I have to go on, the less I can promise." He got up from his seat and motioned for Gabe to remain. "Let me check my sources. I'll return in a moment."

With that, Zachariah left the room, closing the door after he left.

Gabe looked around the room, wondering what he could discover about his host while the man was absent.

Everyone has a secret if you know where to look, he mused.

He searched the small room but could find nothing. There was nothing in the space aside from the table and the chairs surrounding it—no doors to other chambers, no other furniture, nothing.

"Come on, there's got to at least be a hidden floorboard or something," he muttered to himself as he went around, testing several of them with his foot.

He found nothing. Not a loose brick in the walls nor a floorboard that seemed hollow. It seemed this Zachariah fellow had nothing to hide. He didn't get very long to conduct his search before he heard the tell-tale signs of the doorknob creaking. He hastily returned to his chair and resumed his previous position.

A moment later, his host came through the door, closing it behind him. He was alone.

"She's a member of the Eagle's Claw Clan," he said slowly, his head low.

"Really?" Gabe replied. "*Scheisse*! Those people are damn near impossible to track down."

Zachariah nodded. "Very true. She likely returned to

her home base to report in after she found her cover had been compromised."

"Ugh." Gabe rolled his eyes. "Just my luck. She would go to the one place no one can find."

"Well," Zachariah offered. "Perhaps not no one."

Gabe's ears perked up. "Oh? Do you have an inkling, perchance?"

The big man shook his head. "Alas, no. But if anyone does know where it is, it would be the Master. He knows more than any of us, and his spy network is much better connected than even mine."

"Ugh," Gabe said again. "I just saw him recently, too. If I go to him again so soon, he'll know something is up."

Zachariah shrugged. "It's your only chance. Sorry I couldn't be of more help."

Gabe got up, crossed over to Zachariah, and clapped him once on the back. "Well, you gave it your best shot. I guess there's something to be said for that."

The big man got up. "Let me walk you back to the entrance of town," he offered.

Gabe waved him off with a hand. "No need. I'll see myself out."

The Master strode into his magical laboratory with his head held high. He was in a good mood today, which was rare for him. Given how his research had been going lately, he had no reason to be dour.

He walked through the entryway and closed the door behind him, then flicked on the magitech lights that rimmed the walls. They came on almost instantly, illuminating the dark chamber.

What he saw next wiped the grin off his face. A dark man was sitting in the corner of his lab and not a prisoner. Instead, it was someone he knew quite well.

The Master glowered at the individual. The person smiled back at him.

"How nice to see you, Gabriel." The words rolled smoothly off his tongue, giving no hint of the anger that was starting to boil underneath the surface at this intrusion.

No one came into his lab without an invitation. It was one of his few hard and fast rules. Student or no, he would make sure Gabe paid for this. If word got out that someone had broken this most sacred of rules, there would be pandemonium.

He was glad he'd decided to use a disguise today. He usually didn't in the lab, but he was wearing the body of a nondescript male, middle-aged, with brown hair and eyes, and a slight limp on the right foot. His clothes were a simple gray made of unassuming wool fabric. To the passerby, he would look like any other servant.

"I assure you, the pleasure is all mine," Gabe replied. His smile broadened as he spoke.

The Master kept staring at him, not willing to take his eyes off his visitor for even a second. "What brings you down here at this hour? I do not recall summoning you."

Gabe nodded. "That's true, you didn't. Worry not, it's little more than a social call."

"Indeed," the Master replied, though he knew it would

be anything but. Gabe was unpredictable at times, but he wasn't sociable.

"So," he continued. "What can I do to make your stay more pleasant today? Come to watch me work?"

His visitor chuckled. "Something like that." He ran his fingers through his dusty-blond hair. "Actually, I came for a little chat. I was hoping you might have some information for me."

The Master's ears perked up. Now there was an unusual request. Gabe came for power, not information. Whatever he wanted, it must be important. One corner of his lips curled upward, giving the impression of a snarl. "I'd be happy to give you whatever information I have. You know that, child."

"Great!" Gabe replied. "I'm looking for someone. An elderly woman who goes by the name of Valerie. Turns out, she belongs to the Eagle's Claw Clan, and no one seems to know where she went."

That earned a slight eyebrow raise from the Master. How unusual for Gabe of all people to be looking for one of the enemies. He usually never bothered with such things, preferring internal political games.

"So sorry to hear that she's gone missing," he responded. "A shame that."

Gabe nodded again. "Hmm. Yes, a true shame." He took a step closer. "You see, I was hoping you might know where their base of operations is. I'm certain an individual at your level would know where to find them."

The Master rubbed his chin thoughtfully for a second. "Hmm, yes, you would think so, wouldn't you. Alas, not even I know the location of their base."

His visitor looked surprised for a half-second, then it was gone, replaced with that stupid grin of his. "Really? I would have thought for sure you'd know."

"If I knew where their base was, it wouldn't be their base any longer. If you know what I mean."

"Ah, I believe I do," Gabe said. He bobbed his head once more in affirmation. He took a few steps back and sank into a nearby chair.

The Master scowled. That was his favorite chair. How dare Gabe use it.

"Anyway, since I'm here and all, any news on the research front?" Gabe asked, stretching and putting his feet up in the process.

The Master thought for a second before answering. He took another look at Gabriel, defiling his chair, and almost killed him. Instead, his lips curled into a full smile. "Perhaps," he replied. "Perhaps I might know a thing or two."

Gabe's eyes brightened, and he snapped out of the chair. "You do!" he insisted. "You have made some sort of progress! I knew it!"

"Now, now." The Master waved him off with a dismissive hand motion. "I said perhaps. I've made some slight gains here and there. Let me show you."

He reached out a hand and gingerly touched Gabriel with one bare finger, and concentrated. A wave of pure energy flowed into him, making him feel rejuvenated.

Gabe, for his part, collapsed to his knees under the Master's touch. The man choked on his own spit for a second and grabbed frantically at his chest. Then, as quickly as the sensation had come, it left him.

His visitor took a full minute before he was successful

in standing. He dusted himself off and looked at the Master with renewed respect. "That was something, all right," he said at last.

The Master nodded. "Yes, well, I did say I might know a thing or two, didn't I?"

Gabe went back over to the chair and sat down. "So, does it only work with direct contact?"

He nodded once. "For now, yes," he admitted. "But, I hope to have perfected the art soon. However…"

"Yes, Master?" Gabe's eyes had grown bright in anticipation.

"Well, the thing is, I need more test subjects. A lot more. My current stockpile just isn't cutting it. I need fresh recruits, full of vim and vigor," the Master explained.

Gabe's ears perked up. "Oh?"

He kept going. "I have an idea where to get some, but it would take a shrewd mind with great talent to accomplish it."

"I'm listening," Gabe replied.

It was obvious his visitor thought the Master was talking about him. How fortunate. "The Stratton operation. It's been dormant ever since the unfortunate incident with Severin. I'm sure you're well familiar with that."

Gabe nodded. "Indeed."

"Good." The Master clapped his hands together. "I need someone to restart the Stratton operation. Except this time, I want them to take a more…hands-on approach to things—no more sitting on the sidelines. I want you to infiltrate the city and take it over proper. Can you do that?"

His visitor appeared lost in thought for a moment. At

long last, he inclined his head. "Yes, I think I can. I'll need troops, though."

"Of course. You can have whatever troops are still available from Severin's branch. They're not doing much at the moment. I trust that's all you'll need. The city's defenses are weak, and half the guard already works for us."

There was a greedy look in Gabriel's eyes. The Master wondered what was going on in that mind of his.

"Consider it done. And then?"

The Master gave him a cold, dark smile. "Then you'll start bringing me willing test subjects by the cartload. Feel free to have your pick of the populace. I don't really care who they are, so long as they're full of vitality."

For a brief second, a strange look passed over Gabe's features. It might have been doubt or uncertainty, but it was gone too quickly to know for sure.

"Done," Gabe said after a moment's pause. "But in return, you'll do your best to find that hidden base for me."

The Master waved dismissively. "Easily. I'm already working on it, I assure you. Now leave me be. I have many studies to attend to today, and I'm already behind schedule."

"Of course, Master. I wish you the best of luck with your...studies."

With that, Gabriel got up, patted him once on the shoulder, and walked out the door.

The Master waited several minutes to make sure that his guest was long gone before doing anything. He even used his magic to search for the man's presence to be certain. To his relief, the man had been good to his word. He was no longer in the Dusk Raven stronghold.

He wasn't sure how Gabriel had managed to learn his way around the base so well, but that was of little consequence at the moment. He had other, more pleasurable things to focus his attention on today.

But first, he had one more little errand to take care of.

"Daniel?" he called. He knew his trusted servant wouldn't be far away, but he both spoke the word out loud and used mental magic to call him at the same time, just in case.

A moment later, his servant appeared at the doorway. The Master smiled at him.

"Yes, Master?" Daniel asked.

"Remind me, Daniel, to have Gabriel killed next time he sets foot in this stronghold," the Master ordered calmly.

Daniel nodded. "Of course, Master. It will be done."

There, that was settled. Now he could finally focus on his studies in peace and quiet.

CHAPTER ELEVEN

Sariah woke with a start. She wasn't sure what time it was, but she was safe and sound in her own bed in Talon's Reach. She'd had enough of waking up in strange beds to last a lifetime.

Her eyes darted around the small room, trying to figure out what might have woken her. Nothing looked out of place. Everything was exactly where it belonged. She got up to search through her belongings carefully just to make sure.

It didn't take very long, seeing as she didn't have a lot of possessions. Pretty much just what she'd brought with her that she'd been allowed to keep, and the few extra items the clan had given her. Still, she checked everything anyway.

She rummaged through her belongings. Her few changes of clothes were folded and sitting nicely in her small dresser. Her shoes were underneath the clothes. There was a fresh leather patch on her shoe to cover the spot where the needle had poked through on the way in.

The only other things she had to her name were her

handful of weapons—a sword and a couple of knives, including Lucien's dagger.

She wondered for perhaps the hundredth time why she'd never gotten rid of that thing. It had been responsible for killing her parents. Why would she want such an awful artifact to remain so close to her?

She'd used it to kill him, so there was that. In an odd way, it was all she had left to connect herself to her parents, now that she'd donated her brooch to the clan. She supposed that had something to do with it.

Sariah rubbed her eyes a few times and had resolved to go back to bed when she heard a slight scuffling noise coming from outside her door.

That's odd, she thought. No one is ever up and about after curfew.

A small part of her wanted to check it out to see what the fuss was about. She'd always been the curious sort. It was her curiosity that had gotten her wrapped up in this mess to begin with.

She laid down on her bed and decided to ignore it. Whatever someone was up to outside didn't have anything to do with her. She could let it go.

But the noise came again, even closer. And then again. It was coming from practically right outside her door.

Wrinkling her nose, she got up. She pulled on the shoulders of her nightgown to make sure she was properly covered up and walked over to the door. She still wasn't going to take part in whatever was happening, but she would at least tell them to knock it off so she could get some sleep.

Sariah waited until she heard the strange noise again,

then she thrust open the door and looked in the hallway beyond. Only nothing was there. She blinked and rubbed her eyes and looked again, but there was still nothing.

"What the heck?" she asked the air around her.

Shaking her head, she went back inside and shut the door, then laid down on her bed. She must have been hearing things.

As if on cue, the noise came again.

Sariah growled, got back up, and marched over to the door. She swung it wide open once again like she was daring whatever was on the other side to come and get her. There was nothing.

"Probably some stupid little kid playing around with an invisibility spell," she muttered. It would certainly explain why she couldn't see them.

Satisfied with her explanation, she went back into her room and tried to ignore the noises. Within a few moments, they were gone, and she was left alone with her thoughts once again.

Yawning, she tried to fall asleep but found that she could not. The pleasure of sleep was proving to be elusive this warm autumn evening.

So, she sat on the edge of the bed and stretched, trying to clear her mind.

That was proving difficult, too. She was still reeling a bit from her loss to Will when he'd fought her with two blades.

Sariah had held her own for a few minutes, then Will had beaten her handily. He had made it look like he wasn't even trying. Maybe he hadn't been. It had been a sound beating that had shaken her confidence in her own abilities.

Maybe I should try the two-blade method, she thought for the dozenth time. She kept meaning to ask Will to train her in it, but then promptly forgot when the time came to actually do so. She resolved to ask him before training tomorrow, although part of her worried it would only make her skill even worse.

Angry at herself for getting down on her abilities and for her seeming inability to get any real sleep tonight, she decided to try going for a walk. Perhaps the walk and the fresh air would help her clear her mind.

She fetched her shoes and a good, solid pair of breeches and put them on, then walked over to her door once more. This time, she opened it slowly and softly, hoping not to disturb anyone.

With the earlier ruckus, she hadn't been too concerned about someone calling her out for being out after curfew, but now that it was calm, it was a very real possibility. She wasn't sure what the punishment was for being out after curfew, but she wasn't eager to find out, either.

Once she'd cleared the door, her eyes trailed up and down the hallway, searching for signs of other people. She didn't find anyone.

Breathing a small sigh of relief, she let her door close behind her, once again making sure it moved softly and slowly so as not to cause a disruption, then she started walking.

At first, she wasn't sure which direction she wanted to go. All she knew was that she wanted some peace and quiet and a little fresh air to clear her head. But soon, she recognized that the path she was on would lead her right to the training courtyard.

She giggled at herself. Somehow, she should have known that even her feet would betray her.

Might as well get in some extra practice since I'm down here anyway. I need all the training I can get if I'm to protect everyone.

Sariah strode up to the weapons rack and pulled out her favorite practice blade. It was a quarter of a hand shorter than most of the other practice weapons, which made it a good length and weight for her.

Will had told her that picking the right weapon was half the battle.

Pick a sword that's too short or too heavy, and you'll spend more time overcompensating for it than you will sticking it in your opponent, she mused in his voice.

It was another of Will's rules. He had dozens of rules. That one was rule eight, she thought. She marveled that she'd managed to memorize all of them in such a short time. Of course, he drilled them into her several times a day, so it wasn't that shocking.

Sariah gave the blade a practice swing to warm up her muscles. It felt natural in her hand. More natural than her own personal sword. She guessed that it was because she practiced with it so often.

A blade is not a weapon. It's an extension of your own arm. You are the weapon, she repeated in her mind. That was rule nine.

She shook her head to clear phantom Will out of her brain and gave the blade a few more practice swings. She took care to warm up slowly, lest she pull something. No doubt, she'd have another training session in the morning. She wanted to make sure she was in good shape for it.

Right as she was moving in between lunges and sweeping blows, she heard a strange commotion from the far side of the courtyard.

Her blood froze, and she stopped swinging the blade. She strained to see what was going on. Someone had a light, and she could make out the hazy shapes of a couple of people talking about something, but not much else.

It's probably nothing, she thought. At the very least, nothing that I should be concerned about.

She tried to ignore them, but their motions were quite animated so she ended up watching them for a few moments, despite the potential danger. If whoever it was caught wind of her watching after curfew, she'd be punished for sure. But then, why were they out here at this hour? What were they doing out so late? They would get in trouble, too.

If something was so important they could only discuss it in the dead of night, it must be something pretty cool.

Sariah shook her head. She had no business over there. She gently replaced her practice weapon on the shelf and started to walk away.

Just then, the conversation on the other side of the field began to get heated, and one of the voices grew loud. She could make out a few words, something about a secret battle plan.

That piqued her curiosity quite a bit. In spite of herself, Sariah found she was walking toward the noise instead of away from it.

What am I doing? She shook her head and stopped

moving. Though, of course, she already knew the answer. She was snooping, and even though it was none of her business, she desperately wanted to know more.

She shrugged. She might as well find out what all the fuss was about.

When she got closer, she had the forethought to cast an invisibility spell so no one would be able to see her skulking about. She still had no desire to get caught.

Once she was close enough, she could make out who the voices belonged to, along with what was being said. One of the voices belonged to Will.

What's he doing up at this hour? she wondered. And who was he arguing with?

That answer came soon enough. It took her a moment to place the other voice since she hadn't heard it as often, but those calm, icy tones could only belong to one person—Ilene. Will was having an argument with Ilene.

Now Sariah really had to know what it was about. Those two never argued, at least, not in public. Whatever they were arguing about, it must be vitally important for them to be doing it at this hour.

She craned her neck to better make out the words.

"It's simply not worth the risk," one voice said. That was Ilene.

"Bah! Of course, it is! We're going to need to take some risks if we're to win this war. This is one of those risks!" Will said, practically yelling at her.

Sariah still didn't know what they were arguing about, but she loved getting a closer look at their interpersonal relationship. Those two must be more intimate than she thought to talk to each other like that. She wiped a small grin from her face and listened.

Will let out a huge sigh. "Look, we need all the help we can get. You saw what happened at the Battle of Overlook. We got our arses handed to us back there. Surely you can realize that."

"Yes, I am well aware of that unfortunate incident," Ilene countered. Her voice sounded a bit heated but still refined.

"We lost some good men in that excursion," Will continued. "Bruce, Andrew, Lee. Good, hard-working, well-trained men."

Ilene sighed. "I am certain you did not call me out of bed at this hour to remind me of our past mistakes, William."

Will let out a slight growl. "No, ma'am, no, I did not."

Nothing was said for a moment. No one said anything, and the outlines didn't move. Then finally, Will broke the silence. "Look, I've been working with these new recruits for weeks now. They're honest men and women, they are, but they're just not at the same level."

The outline of Will took a step closer to Ilene. He put one hand on his head and pulled downward. "And I'll be honest with you, my lady. They might not ever be."

Ilene's outline took a step backward and sat down in a nearby chair. "What are you trying to tell me, Will? Exactly, I mean. Spell it out for me."

Will sighed again and took another step closer to Ilene. "I'm not sure how to say this, my lady, but unless we find some new recruits soon that are way better than the current stock, we may not have many other options."

Ilene's outline threw one hand up in the air in exasperation. "What about that new girl, Sariah? She seems promising enough. She actually passed the trial."

Sariah furrowed her brow when she heard that. Was she supposed to have lost against Will on that first day? She was thoroughly confused but ignored it to keep snooping. They had to get back to the good part eventually.

"Aye, that she did," Will offered. "And she's a damn fine recruit, too. Easily the best we have right now. But she's only one girl. Surely you can't expect one lone girl to face down the whole of the Dusk Raven army, can you?"

Sariah beamed. Will was complimenting her again, and to Ilene at that! She decided she liked it when he complimented her. It was far better than his constant string of insults.

"No, of course not. I wasn't saying that," Ilene countered. Sariah imagined her rolling her eyes, even though such a motion was totally unlike her. "I was merely pointing out that if there's one recruit such as her, there could be more."

Will growled again. He obviously didn't like where she was going. "Oh, come now, my lady! You can't believe that. She's one in a hundred. Maybe even more! Besides, anyone with even half an ounce of talent is more likely to sign up with the Dusk Ravens than us. They'll have a better chance at a future, there. Everyone knows that!"

"Well, I don't," Ilene said in a huff.

The outline of Will rubbed its forehead. "Of course, I didn't mean everyone, my lady. I'm sorry for the outburst."

Ilene's outline raised one hand gingerly and placed it on Will's arm. "I know you didn't, my dear William. It's okay."

My dear William? Sariah thought. This conversation was getting better by the moment.

"At any rate, that's why we're in this predicament, and why I made this recommendation. We need more than just people. We need an edge. This find gives us a solid edge."

Ilene backed up a bit. "You really think it wise? How many good, hard-working, well-trained men will we lose to this cause?"

Will let out another sigh. "I don't know. Three or four, maybe. Hopefully, not more than that. The prize won't be very well guarded while it's in transit. It's a perfect opportunity to strike!"

"You complain about lost men, and you think the best way to improve our situation is to lose some more? I do not understand your logic, William."

Will threw his hands up. "When you put it that way, I agree with you."

There was a nod from Ilene. "I'm glad we're finally able to see eye to eye, then."

Will took another step forward. There was barely any distance between their outlines now. "But only when you put it like that!" he spat. "This is a good move—a wise course of action. Yes, we might lose a few more men, but we will gain so much in return! Our other troops will fare so much better with this technology!"

Ilene backed away and looked a little defensive. Sariah figured she might be a little scared by Will's sudden advance. She put a hand up in defense. "I appreciate your zeal," she said, "but that doesn't mean I necessarily agree with your conclusion."

"Just let me explain the whole plan in detail. Maybe then, you'll see my side of things."

Ilene let out another sigh. Her outline made a grand flourish with one hand. "Very well, go ahead and explain the plan."

Will rubbed his hands together and stood up straighter. "Thank you, my lady. You won't regret this!"

She imagined he had a big grin on his face as he went over the next part.

"There's a caravan on its way up from the southern regions right now as we speak. Our scouts say they have maybe eight to ten men at most guarding the item in question. Current movement patterns place them about two days' solid march west of our location right now."

Will paused for a moment before continuing. "Right now, they're about as far away from any Dusk Raven outposts as they'll ever be. If we strike now, they won't be able to signal for reinforcements. It's a prime target and an incredible opportunity."

Ilene raised a finger to her lips. "Won't the Dusk Ravens notice that their caravan never makes it to its intended destination? If they trace the attackers back, they could find our location. Then we'll all be dead."

Will was waving his hands around. "Nonsense! They'd have no way to do that. We can dispose of the bodies long before anyone could stumble upon them. They'll never know where the attack happened, let alone where they came from!"

"Still, it's too dangerous," Ilene insisted. She let out another sigh. "I'm just not sure I'm ready to commit the amount of force it would require and sentence a few good men to their deaths. I cannot have that on my conscience."

"But my lady—"

The Eagle's Claw leader held up a hand to silence Will. "But nothing. We will not talk about this any further tonight. Tomorrow, perhaps, but not tonight. The hour grows late. I wish to speak of...other matters."

Will bowed his head. "Yes, my lady."

The two lowered their voices then and started speaking to one another in hushed tones. Sariah bent forward to try and hear what the two were saying, but she couldn't make it out. Whatever it was, it sounded pleasant, not heated like their earlier discussion.

Just then, Sariah heard a noise from off to her left. It startled her almost enough to make her fall face-forward into the dirt, but she managed to steady herself just in time. She looked around, trying to locate the source of the strange noise. She caught a flicker of movement, then it was gone.

A chill ran up her spine. Had someone caught her? That should be impossible since she'd been using an invisibility spell. Still, if someone had… She had to find out for sure.

Sariah turned to fully face the direction of the noise and started moving forward. There was nothing that she could see, but there was a bend in the path not far ahead, and whoever it was could have ducked around it.

That strange noise came again, from somewhere behind the wall in front of her. It sounded like a child giggling. If that could even be believed at this late hour.

She bounded forward the next few steps and rounded the bend quickly, as quietly as she was able, and came face to face with a little girl. It was the same girl who had been cheering her on the day before in the courtyard.

The little thing was staring right through her, and she had a look of mirth in her eyes.

Sariah wondered for a moment why she hadn't startled the young girl. Then she remembered she had cast the invisibility spell. Of course the girl couldn't see her. She dropped the spell, and in the same instant the young girl let out a surprised gasp and ran a few steps away.

"It's okay, little girl," Sariah insisted in a whisper. She held out a hand in the young girl's direction. "I won't hurt you, I promise."

The young maiden peeked out from behind her hands and stared at Sariah for a moment, then buried her face in her hands again. She didn't seem convinced.

"I promise I won't tell anyone you were out after curfew," Sariah offered. She hoped that would do the trick. The girl would want to avoid punishment.

This time, the young girl raised her head up a little bit longer and lowered her hands ever so slightly. Sariah caught a hint of her soft, blue eyes through strands of midnight hair.

Still, though, the little girl didn't budge.

Sariah beckoned for her to move forward. "Come on," she said. "I won't bite. Promise. I'm Sariah. I'm new here. Who are you?"

The young girl took a few hesitant steps forward but remained quiet.

"That's it," Sariah continued. "Were you attracted to the big yellow light and all the yelling in the tent?"

The young girl nodded once.

Sariah smiled broadly. "Me too. I came to watch. I like intense scenes like that. Like people fighting, or...or battles with weapons. You like those, too, don't you?"

Another nod and the girl took another couple of small steps forward.

"Yeah, I bet you do. I saw you watching me the other day. Thank you for rooting for me. It meant a lot."

That seemed to do the trick. The young girl's eyes brightened, and she gained enough courage to walk forward and touch Sariah's outstretched palm.

"What's your name, little girl?"

"H-heather," the young maiden said in a voice barely over a whisper.

Sariah flashed her another grin. "Heather? That's a very lovely name. I like it a lot."

"You do?" Heather asked. She tilted her head to the side.

"Mmhmm." Sariah nodded. "It's a very pretty name."

Heather preened a little and swayed side to side. She beamed up at Sariah. "It's my birthday today, Sariah."

Sariah bent to her level. "It is?" Another quick nod. "That's so exciting." She pinched the little girl's cheek. "How old are you today?"

"Eight." Heather puffed out her chest as much as she could and gave Sariah a giant grin.

"Wow? Eight years old. You must be very big, Heather." She ruffled the little girl's hair with one of her hands as she spoke.

"Yep! I can already wield a sword, just like you!" She made a few slicing motions with one of her hands and did a pretend lunge forward.

Sariah watched the girl, enchanted, and tried not to

critique her form. Will's training had taken quite the toll on her, she decided, for her to even think about critiquing a little girl wielding a pretend weapon. Instead, she smiled at the girl and gave her a little nudge.

"Come, Heather," she said, holding out her hand. "We should get you back to your mommy."

"Oh, I don't have a mommy," Heather explained. Her face drooped and the color seeped out of her cheeks.

"That's okay," Sariah offered, flashing the young girl a smile. "I don't, either."

"Really?" There was a hint of brightness in the girl's eyes again.

"Really," Sariah affirmed with a nod. "But surely you have someone who takes care of you."

Heather nodded. "I do. It's my—"

"There you are!" a hurried voice interrupted them from the right. It was a voice that Sariah would have recognized anywhere. Her whole face brightened.

"Valerie!" Sariah shouted.

The elderly woman stopped in her tracks and looked down at Heather, then up at Sariah, then back down at Heather. In the end, she threw her arms wide open.

"Sariah! Heather! Come here, both of you!" she insisted.

They both obliged her.

"I thought you might have been killed after all you did for me!" Sariah admitted, tears running down her cheeks. She saw a glint of similar tears on Valerie's face.

Valerie pushed her away a bit and stared at her. "Oh, it's going to take a lot more than that to get me down. I'm just glad you were able to find us. They didn't give you too much trouble, I hope?"

Sariah thought back over the past month of torture and virtual hell that Will had put her through, but in the end, she shook her head. "Nope."

"That's good. I'm so glad."

"Me too. I'm glad you're safe."

The two hugged again for a moment until Heather tugged at Sariah's shirt to get her attention. "This is my gamma, Valerie," she beamed.

"Your gamma?" She looked down at Heather then up at Valerie and giggled slightly. Valerie laughed, too.

"Sure am," Valerie admitted with a smile. "I wouldn't trade it for the world."

Sariah gave them both a big grin. She was happy that Valerie hadn't died on her account. She'd been worried about that for a while.

"Well, you two should probably get back to your quarters before someone finds you out after curfew," Sariah said at last.

Valerie looked down at Heather. The older woman looked like she had at least a dozen things she wanted to say right then and there, but in the end, she simply nodded.

"Come, little one," Valerie said. "Let's let Sariah get some sleep."

Sariah watched the two walk hand in hand for a moment before doing anything. Part of her wished her life was still that simple, but alas, it wasn't meant to be.

Instead, her life had just gotten a whole lot more complicated. She wasn't supposed to have overheard the conversation between Ilene and Will, but now that she had, she couldn't stop thinking of it.

A technology prize that could put the Eagle's Claw over

the top? How could they not go after it? And yet, Ilene was so hesitant. She couldn't put her troops in danger. Sariah could respect that.

She paced, letting the thoughts ruminate in her mind.

But what if Ilene didn't have to? Sariah could do it for them. With her new training and confidence, she could take on a half dozen men, especially with the element of surprise on her side.

In her mind, a plan was forming. Suddenly, she knew just how to help Eagle's Claw and gain Will's favor in one fell swoop.

CHAPTER TWELVE

Harvey slowly pried open one of his eyelids. He took a peek at his surroundings. It was dark and musty, with only a dim torchlight in the distance giving off any hint of where he was.

The area around him slowly came into focus. He was in the middle of a rough-hewn stone hallway. Behind him stood a heavy steel door. The same one he'd teleported past on his way out of the mines.

A wave of relief washed over him, and he breathed a heavy sigh. He was back within the relative safety and obscurity of the mines, and in his hands was the key to the townspeople's freedom.

Somehow, his plan had worked.

He didn't rejoice, instead he decided to play it overly cautious. He went up to the door and pressed his ear to it for any sounds that might indicate knowledge of the mission he'd carried out just moments before, like the sound of an alarm and soldiers buzzing to and fro.

He listened for perhaps a solid minute, but heard nothing. He couldn't even hear the faint sound of the guard named Freddie snoring away on the other side.

Smiling softly to himself, he figured that was probably because the thick steel would mute such soft tones.

Harvey felt better. He had accomplished his mission, and no one out there was the wiser. At least not yet. The next time one of the guard shifts was sent in to move the chained up miners, or the next time someone inspected the fake key he'd left behind, the jig would be up. It was Harvey's intention not to wait that long. He aimed to make his move as soon as possible.

Whistling an old tune from his childhood as he went, he sauntered down the darkened mine corridor, head held high. No one was up here, so he made his way uninterrupted.

Reaching the elevator, he quickly maneuvered its parts like he'd done on so many previous occasions practically without thinking about it. His mind was consumed with escape plans and ensuring everyone got out of the mine in one piece.

Everyone but the guards that is. He couldn't care less about them. If the mine foreman was secretly a Dusk Raven, it was a good bet that most of the guards were, too. That took them from bystander status all the way down to worthless scum. He could kill them without a moment's pause.

The elevator reached the bottom of the shaft with a slight thud. He wound his way through passages, both old and new. Once he was within earshot of his people, he made the sound of a bird call.

It was their previously agreed-upon signal. A moment

later a gruff voice, most likely Padron's, made the same bird call back.

Harvey smiled. His people had been unharmed while he was out. This night was getting better and better.

"Padron!" Harvey called. "I'm back!"

"Ye better have brought some fine ale back with ya, lad!" Padron answered.

Harvey rounded the last corner and gave his friend a big hug. "No, but I've got something even better." He held up the dark iron key. It glimmered slightly in the dim light of the passageway.

Padron's eyes lit up like a child on his birthday. "Well, I'll be damned. Ya did it ya son of a bitch."

"Shall we see if it works?" Harvey asked. The rearick bobbed his head fiercely.

Harvey took the key and placed it in the thick lock. It slid in easily. He tried to give it a turn, but it didn't want to budge. Frowning, he put a little more force into it. It took a lot more effort than he would have thought possible, but before long, the key turned and he heard a loud click.

Both of them stared down at the chains in awe. The lock was undone. Padron was free.

The rearick kicked off the manacle from his leg and rubbed it several times to return feeling to the appendage. His leg had a nasty scar on it that was red around the edges, but at that moment, he didn't seem to care.

"Ahh, it feels good ta be free again, lad," Padron admitted. His eyes darted around the long corridor. "Let's go free the others."

Harvey nodded. He put out one hand to stop the very excited rearick. "Wait," he said. "Did you tell them about the plan? Do they know what to do once they're free?" he asked.

Padron nodded. "Aye, lad. They know not to act suspicious." He paused for a moment. "It'll be hard for them, lad. They've been trapped for far longer than we have. If any of them make a move anyways, just go easy on them, eh?"

Harvey flashed him a dopey grin. "I understand. Still, that'll make it that much harder on the rest of us."

"Aye, it will, lad. But ya get what ya get."

"Very well." His head bobbed in agreement. "Let's just get this over with."

He moved to the next person in line. It was Justine, one of the rearick who had helped him get into the mines in the first place. He gave her a sheepish grin. It was his fault she was trapped in here like this with her friend Bailey, who was chained a few feet farther down the wall.

If only I'd been smarter about it all back then, he thought glumly. It wasn't as though he'd had any reason to suspect the mine would be under this heavy of a guard.

This time, the key worked quickly and required little effort. Justine's lock didn't seem to be in as bad a shape as Padron's. He looked up at Justine, and she smiled at him and batted her eyelashes.

"Why thank ye, kind gentleman," she said.

Harvey blushed. Was she hitting on him, here of all places? He shook his head. It didn't matter. He had no time for such thoughts. There were dozens of people to unchain, and only one key to do it with.

Worse, he had to have them all free and in place before the next mealtime for his plan to work. Time was of the essence.

He flashed her a grin and ducked his head, then moved on to the next prisoner. Down the line he went, working the locks as quickly as he could. Most of them moved freely enough. Only a few gave him any real trouble.

Soon enough, everyone was free. Everyone was happier without their chains, and thankfully none of them did anything stupid.

Harvey's eyes looked upward for a moment. "How long until mealtime?" he asked.

"About an hour, if me tum's any indication," Padron replied. He patted his round belly for good measure.

Harvey chuckled. He gave Padron's belly a swift, friendly swat. "It's a good thing we have that to go by."

Padron burst out in laughter, and a few of the towns-folk joined in. The rearick's appetite was known far and wide, and having lived off meager rations for the past few weeks, he probably was well and truly starving.

"Let's get you that meal," Harvey offered. He looked around the room. "All right everyone, get to your places." He looked at two rather stout individuals. "You and you. You're with Padron. Make sure that belly of his doesn't get us into any trouble," he added with a wink.

Padron's cheeks reddened, then they all burst out into laughter again. It was good to be free.

Harvey was waiting at the door to the mine, tapping his foot impatiently. The food run was a good half hour overdue.

He wondered if they'd been found out.

There was no way to be certain, of course, but it was possible. If they had, he figured the guards would come rushing in. They were armed. If you call a handful of pickaxes armed, then his people were too. Even still, most of them had no idea how to use them as weapons. The guards would have the upper hand in any face to face confrontation.

Which was why it was his plan to ensure there were as few of those as possible. He tapped his foot again, then started pacing around the small area.

Just where are those stupid guards, anyway?

A moment later, he heard the sound of metal creaking on metal as a key turned in the door, then the handle started to slowly move.

Harvey took a deep breath to calm his nerves and put on a worried expression. The better part of his plan depended on what happened in the next few minutes. If he was successful, then most of them would make it out safely. If not...he preferred not to think about that.

A rather large guard was the first one to come through the crack in the door. He was holding a dusty looking bag that had patches sewn on in several spots. Behind him was another guard carrying a medium-sized barrel of water.

That was their rations and water for the morning. Old, dried food in a dusty bag that had clearly seen better days and some rainwater in an oily barrel. He knew it all too well, having lived off it for the last weeks.

Harvey didn't wait. He pulled on the tunic of the lead guard until the man was looking straight at him. He did his best to make his eyes look wild and spoke fast.

"There you are! Come quickly! There was an accident

in the corridor below! Comfry and half a dozen of the other miners were injured!"

It was a lie, of course, but it was a reasonable one. In between the heavy equipment, large amount of rocks, and the small number of explosives they had down there, it was entirely plausible an accident would occur eventually.

The main guard looked concerned. If Harvey didn't know better, he'd swear the man cared about his prisoners. But he'd seen the look of disdain in the man's eyes on countless occasions before this.

"Come on, man!" Harvey whined. He pulled harder on the man's tunic as if to lead him down the hallway.

The guard brushed off Harvey's hand and pushed him away. Harvey let himself fall to the ground to add a little extra oomph to the act. When he heard the guard sigh, he knew it was working.

"Please!" Harvey pleaded. He had a fake tear coming out of the corner of an eye. "Comfry's my dad. I can't bear to lose him!"

It was another lie, but there was no way this guard could know that.

The big guard seemed a little shaken. He looked behind him to the man standing lazily at attention at the mine entrance. "You there!" he shouted gruffly. "Get me some stretchers and another dozen guards. We've got a mess to clean up!" he demanded.

The guard standing outside the mine snapped to attention and saluted, then ran off quickly.

"Now," said the big guard, turning his attention back to Harvey. "Where are these injured miners?"

Harvey tried his best not to smile. He worked his face

into a terrified frown and lowered his head to look scared. Scraping his feet, he answered. "They're in the new mineshaft at the bottom. I'll take you to them."

The big guard rolled his eyes and sighed, then beckoned with one of his gloved hands. "Lead the way."

Comfry looked around the abandoned mineshaft. Where there had once been at least two dozen miners toiling were now abandoned tools and piles of rubble. It was a stark, lonely scene, though he knew it wouldn't remain that way for long.

Not that what was to come would be that much better, but he had agreed to his fate, so there was nothing he could do about it now.

He looked down at his leg. There was a rather large rock hovering precariously over it. It was in such a position as to look like it was pressing down on his leg, trapping him in place, though in reality, it was doing nothing of the sort.

The whole scene was a prop, and he, the lone actor being given a last chance to hold the performance of a lifetime.

Oh, there had been arguments, of course. Harvey had insisted they pull straws or names out of a hat or something to see who got the short straw. He'd even offered to throw his own name in with the lot, though that was utterly ridiculous.

None of the miners would have been given this chance without Harvey's skill and assistance. That young man would make it out of here today, and Comfry would make sure of it the best way he knew how.

He'd always had a bit of a fondness for the young man. Even more so since the kid's mother died and his father had gone off on that good-for-nothing drinking binge of his, forcing his son to pull double shifts at the mines to compensate.

Comfry was glad the boy had a purpose that went well beyond his soul-sucking worthless excuse for a dad. He was proud of the boy.

Never having had his own children, he'd felt like this was the one thing he could do to help Harvey along, and the rest of the town as well. None of the villagers would miss him when he was gone, anyway. Not much, at least. Not like they'd miss Harvey.

Harvey was going places. When the young fool had offered to put his own fate on the line, Comfry had known just what to do.

He wasn't about to let that strong young man throw the rest of his life away. Not when he could do the job just as well. He was old and frail, with few years left on this blasted Irth. He'd made the right call.

Moments later, Comfry heard the sound of movement and hushed whispers from outside the hallway. There were several voices. Dozens, maybe. It seemed Harvey had been successful in luring the guard down here like he'd hoped.

Comfry smiled. Now he was even more sure he'd made the right choice.

"They're in here," a voice called from around the bend. It was Harvey's voice.

Booted feet rushed past Harvey and spilled into the

room. Comfry looked at them, and as he did so, his lips curled upward into a wry smile.

The guards piled in and looked around the room with shocked expressions on their faces. They looked like they'd been duped. It was a look Comfry knew they'd die wearing.

"Welcome!" Comfry shouted over the din of confused whispers.

The guards looked at him.

Comfry held a plunger in his right hand tight and said a quick, silent prayer to the Matriarch and Patriarch. This was the right call. It was the best chance his people had to be safe. Save the many at the expense of the few and all that.

"Welcome," he repeated in a cold voice. His lips curled upward even tighter. "To hell." Then he pressed down hard on the plunger.

The mine foreman woke with a start. He rubbed his eyes and shot out of bed, waking his mistress from the previous night in the process.

Somewhere close by, he could have sworn he'd heard an explosion. But there hadn't been any new demolition work in the mine scheduled for today.

He slapped his mistress on the ass. "Get out of here!" he quipped, smacking her again, harder this time.

"But my clothes!" she whined.

Jeffrey growled and gave her a stink eye. She slunk away, using the bedsheet to hide her skin.

The mine foreman grunted and looked out the small window in his building. It gave him a perfect view of the mine. That was just how he liked it, too. Nothing over there seemed amiss. No one was running around scared or hurried or anything. It was just like any other lazy morning as far as he could tell.

Jeffrey slipped on a pair of pants and headed back over to the bed to sit down. He scanned the floor for a dagger to pick at his teeth but didn't see any. He grunted again, figuring that little bitch of a mistress must have taken his blade with her.

No matter, he'd get it back soon enough. She was on his schedule for the day after tomorrow.

He grinned as he relived the previous night. Marcey was one of his favorites. She liked it a little rough, or at least claimed she did. He didn't really care, so long as she only screamed when he let her.

Just then, he heard another explosion from the direction of the mine. This one was louder than the last.

Jeffrey got up and went back to the window. The door to the mine was wide open. There was a bloody trail on the ground leading away from it toward the large iron door, which sat in a mangled heap on the ground twenty feet away.

The smile on his face faded quickly.

In the same instant, a young guard came rushing into his room. "Humboldt, sir!" the guard cried. "There's been an issue down at the mine!"

"Jeffrey, you twit!" The mine foreman spat back. "I told you to call me by my code name Jeffrey in this town!"

The young guard hung his head low. "Sorry, sir. It won't happen again."

Humboldt, or Jeffrey as he made people call him, shot the kid an icy glare. He had half a mind to behead the kid for the slip-up, but there were more important things to deal with.

He scowled. "Go get my sword ready, you little shit. Then go head down to the mine!"

The young guard gave him a stiff salute. "Right away, sir!" Then he scampered away.

Jeffrey shook his head and scanned the floor for some chest armor. Today was not going to be a good day.

Harvey led the procession of miners in solemn silence. His chest still felt constricted over the loss of Comfry, but he was trying not to think about it. Comfry's sacrifice had meant everyone else's survival.

In his mind, he replayed the scene several times. He couldn't think of another alternative, but that didn't keep him from second-guessing himself. He was determined not to let anyone else suffer a similar fate.

His thoughts were interrupted when they reached the entryway of the mine. Much to Harvey's chagrin, the door leading to outside, and freedom for all of them, was locked shut.

This time, he knew he didn't have the key.

"*Scheisse!*" he swore. "The guards must have locked the door behind them!"

Padron put a big hand on his shoulder. "It's okay, lad. Ye

did tha best ye could," he said. The rearick sighed once and shrugged. "Besides, after that explosion, I'm sure they'll send more people eventually."

Harvey's head bobbed a bit as he pondered that possibility. "True," he admitted. "But then they'll have the drop on us."

I won't let Comfry's sacrifice be in vain, he repeated in his head as he paced the small hallway before the door. But what else can I do?

A moment later, a thought came to him. His eyes lit up, and his face brightened. It was risky, but he had very little time and even fewer options.

"Tell everyone to stand back. Well back," Harvey told Padron, pushing out his hands at the same time.

Padron looked dumbfounded. "What are ye plannin', lad?"

"No time to explain!" Harvey insisted. "Just do it."

The rearick did as he was told. There were a few grumbles from some of the townsfolk as they moved back into the mine, but everyone did as they were bid.

Harvey side-eyed the door. "So this is how it's going to be," he told the massive piece of iron. He cracked his neck. "Fine then. I didn't like you anyway."

Taking a deep breath to calm his nerves, Harvey concentrated. He figured he had one good shot at this, and that was it. Any more than that, and he'd likely not have enough energy left for what came after.

He pulled his hands inward toward his chest and then, in one swift motion, pushed them out toward the door while screaming a battle-cry at the top of his lungs.

A loud booming noise shook the entire hallway as the

heavy iron door flew off its hinges into the area beyond, demolishing everything in its path. Harvey stood with eyes wide, panting and shaking harder than he thought possible. But the deed was done. They were free.

"Well, so much fer the element of surprise," muttered Padron, shaking his head with a massive smile on his face.

Harvey lifted his head up for a moment and flashed him a dopey grin. "I think we kind of lost that when we blew up half the mine, don't you?"

"Ye never were one for subtle measures, were ya?"

They both burst out laughing for a moment before getting serious again. The obstacle blocking their path was gone, but they still needed to get out unscathed.

Harvey shook his head and blinked a few times to clear his eyes of some of the dust. "Everyone, stay behind me. We're getting out!" he shouted. He was greeted by several hoots and hollers from the crowd.

He took a few furtive steps into the outside world. The sun was shining overhead, blinding his sensitive eyes. It was morning, and his eyes hadn't seen real sunlight in so long, it took him several moments to adapt.

Once his eyes had adjusted, he surveyed the carnage that was the mine opening. The massive iron door he'd knocked off its hinges lay in a twisted pile of metal and who knows what else about twenty feet in front of them.

There was a fresh bloodstain on the ground in front of the door, but no sign of a body. Whoever had been guarding the door must have suffered a horrible fate, indeed. Harvey wanted to feel bad for the man but couldn't. The person had most certainly been Dusk Raven scum like the rest of the lot.

Not far off, he caught sight of a sword lying on the ground. Likely the now-dead guard had been wearing it. Harvey picked it up and gave it a few test swings. The blade was lighter than what he was used to, but he could manage. It was better than nothing.

Harvey scanned the horizon. In the distance, about half a dozen men were rushing in their direction. One of them wore ornate armor with a raven emblem on it and carried a sword that looked more decorative than dangerous. The others looked like standard soldiers. They were all coming from the guard complex.

"Huh," Harvey said. "Looks like I did a better job of clearing out the guards than I originally thought."

He turned to face the others. "Run—all of you. You're in no condition to fight. I'll take care of them." He pointed over his shoulder as he spoke.

A sea of stern, grim faces greeted him. Even the women looked angry.

"We're not goin' anywhere, lad," Justine said. Her friend Bailey nodded, as did several of the other miners. "We owe them some payback."

Padron grinned at his fellow rearick, then at Harvey. "It looks like ye got yerself a small army, General."

Harvey looked over the assembled villagers and smiled. There was a tear in his eye, which he quickly wiped away. "Okay," he said at last. "Those of you without a pickaxe, go find some weapons, anything you can use and take on the guards. I'm going after their leader."

The others nodded and started searching. It didn't take long for them to find sticks and other rudimentary implements they could use as clubs and weapons.

Harvey left them to it and turned to face the approaching soldiers. He lowered his sword until it was pointing almost directly at their leader's chest. Even from this distance, Harvey knew who it was, having seen the man's face daily for years.

"Jeffrey!" he cried. "Your reign of terror ends now!" Then he ran.

The mine foreman heard him, for the man broke from the crowd of soldiers and raced toward Harvey.

Harvey's lips curled into a smile. They would all be free soon enough. Just one womanizer and a handful of guards stood in their way now—child's play.

"Eight years!" Jeffrey spat at him as he approached.

Harvey cocked his head to the side but didn't take his attention off the man.

"Eight years I've been in this stupid, one-horse town, running this op." Hatred practically seethed off the man. "I survived everything. The Master's meddling, Lucien, even Severin's fuckup."

Recognition started to dawn on Harvey as the man kept talking. Jeffrey was on him, then, swinging his sword in wide arcs.

He met Jeffrey's blade head-on, swinging his own weapon with enough force to hopefully knock the mine foreman over. Much to his surprise, Jeffrey held his own.

"But you!" Jeffrey continued. "You and your little friends came in here and ruined everything!"

The young man switched the grip on his blade and swung it vertically, then changed it at the last second and went for a broad swipe across Jeffrey's middle. Once more, his attack was thwarted by a deft maneuver from the mine foreman.

Jeffrey's lips curled into a wry smile. "Now, you're going to pay the price."

With that, the older man went into an attack pattern, thrusting and lunging forward with a series of quick strikes.

Harvey deflected them, but he was forced back half a step in the process.

"You're not bad at this," Harvey admitted through labored breaths, bringing his sword up to deflect another blow.

"Heh," Jeffrey replied. He didn't even sound winded. "There's lots you don't know about me, kid."

Feeling's mutual, Harvey thought. He didn't have long to think about it, as a moment later, debris from the entryway came rushing past his head, almost hitting him.

He stole a quick glance behind him to see if it had been a misfire by one of his men, but they were too busy wrestling with the remaining guards. It hadn't been them.

Harvey's eyes narrowed. He looked at Jeffrey with newfound respect, and a little bit of apprehension. "You know magic, too?"

"All the better to kill you with," Jeffrey grunted with a wry grin. He wiggled a couple of fingers on one hand, and another piece of debris picked itself up off the ground and flew toward Harvey.

The young man ducked to avoid the attack just in time, but it left him in a weak position. Jeffrey used that advantage to score a hit on his exposed leg.

Harvey wanted to howl in pain but wasn't about to give

the mine foreman the pleasure. Still, he needed another answer. He seemed to be outclassed in more ways than one at the moment.

He shook off his momentary haze and thought about the situation rationally. He had magic, too, so maybe it was time to start fighting fire with literal fire? Now that was a plan he could get behind.

A smile crept upon his lips as he made a few of his own hand gestures. Moments later, a fireball erupted from his fingers and flew toward the mine foreman.

Jeffrey hastily dodged out of the way, but not in time. His left side came into contact with the fireball and was scorched instantly. The mine foreman fell to the ground.

The smell of burning flesh hung in the air, and Jeffrey clutched his injured side, muttering curses at his attacker. He looked up at Harvey with an odd expression in his eyes.

"Wouldn't kill an injured man, would you?" Jeffrey asked him.

Harvey laughed. "After that speech? Like hell, I wouldn't."

Jeffrey shrugged, then made a desperate lunge with his blade.

Harvey saw the blade coming, but not in time to avoid it, and the blade plunged into his side, leaving a nasty hole.

In retaliation, Harvey summoned forth all the energy he could muster and pushed outward. The effect was intensely gratifying. Jeffrey's body flew through the air much as the iron door had earlier, and landed far away with a loud thud.

Harvey took a deep breath to calm himself and stop the worst of the shaking, then walked over to the mine foreman's body. It wasn't moving, but he raised his blade to strike the man anyway.

Right before his blade made impact, Jeffrey's body disappeared.

Harvey scowled. The mine foreman must have teleported to safety. He would live to see another day, yet.

He had little time to focus on it. The rest of the miners were still in combat. He turned to look at them. They seemed to be holding their own just fine. All of the townsfolk were still standing, whereas only one guard was.

Harvey looked down at his wound. It appeared shallow and too far to the side to have hit any vital organs, which was fortunate. He grabbed at it with one hand and looked back to the battle, scanning for Padron's face.

He found the rearick after a moment and smiled up at him and waved. Padron was half-staring at him, half-engrossed in battle with the last remaining guard. He paused for a moment and flashed Harvey a big grin.

Then Harvey collapsed to the ground, and everything went black.

CHAPTER THIRTEEN

Sariah rubbed her eyes to help rouse herself from her nap. She knew she'd need every ounce of energy she could muster for the upcoming confrontation, so she had decided to take a midday nap to re-energize herself.

It was a risky move, to be sure, taking a nap unguarded out in the open, but if Sariah was honest with herself, risky moves weren't out of character for her. That's why she was alone again, just a few short weeks after finding a whole town's worth of people willing to help her and take her in.

She felt like she was only returning the favor.

That was the excuse she'd kept telling herself. She was helping them by getting them their objective, and at the same time keeping their troops out of harm's way. It was all about the greater good, and this was serving that greater good.

She moaned and sat upright. In all honesty, she wasn't so sure anymore.

Running off on her own to take out a small caravan of Dusk Ravens had seemed like a good idea two nights ago.

Now that she was out in the woods alone, dirty, and shivering from the cold, she was having second thoughts.

It didn't help that today was her seventeenth birthday.

Lowering her head, she let the thought really sink in. Growing up in the poor section of Chatwick like she had after her dad's injury, she hadn't expected a grand celebration for her birthday this year, but she had thought it might be a little bit special.

If nothing else, Harvey would have given her a present. He would have gotten her something impractical like a bracelet or something, saying she needed to be less serious.

Harvey wasn't with her today, and she had no one to blame for that but herself.

Was I wrong to run off without him? she wondered for perhaps the hundredth time. She should have given him the chance to come along.

She shook her head. Thoughts like that wouldn't get her anywhere.

Besides, even if Harvey had agreed to come with her to Talon's Reach, there was no way he would have agreed to this current hair-brained scheme of hers. So either way, she would have been out here in this clearing alone. It was all but inevitable.

Maybe it's my fate to be alone, she thought. I mean, look at my choice in boyfriends, not exactly stellar taste.

She shuddered at the involuntary thought of Gabriel. Despite not wanting to, she still wondered about him quite often and hoped he was doing okay. Even if he was Dusk Raven scum, he'd still been good to her for a time. It was hard to let that go.

Her thoughts turned briefly to what would happen the

next time the two of them met. She wondered if they would still be on opposite sides, or if maybe Gabe would have had a change of heart.

That was probably too much to hope for, she admitted wryly. Still, it was a hope she couldn't quite extinguish.

She rubbed her arms to return some semblance of warmth to them and shook her head to try and clear her thoughts. None of this was going to help her track down that caravan. She needed to stay on target. The Eagle's Claw probably wouldn't even let her back in after this unless she was successful.

Sariah sighed and cast about with her magic, feeling for signs of human life anywhere in the vicinity. There was no guarantee the magic would work. She had no real connection with any of the Dusk Ravens that were supposedly out here, but it was her best bet.

Closing her eyes, she steadied her breathing and concentrated on the spell.

It didn't take long. On the edge of her mind, she felt signs of human life due south of her current position. There were six, or maybe seven people in all. They were right up the road, maybe a thousand meters from her current position.

"That's a little close for comfort," she mused. She was suddenly grateful her nap hadn't gone that well. She didn't want to think what would have happened if they'd stumbled on her while she slept. She shuddered.

She'd been lucky so far, and maybe her luck would hold. She looked up at the sky. It was a little past dusk. The sky was darkening, though the stars weren't visible yet. It was still too light for her to get the jump on them properly. She'd have to wait and hide out somewhere.

After traveling along the path for several minutes, she spotted a small copse of trees off to the side, not far from the path. She made her way there, being careful not to leave a trail for anyone to notice. Hiding would do her no good if she just left a trail for them to follow right to her, after all.

Crouching in the tall grass next to one of the trees, she turned her attention back to the road and waited.

The sky grew fully dark, but there was still no sign of the people she'd sensed earlier.

Did my magic fail me? she wondered. It was possible. She'd made amazing progress in the last weeks, but still had plenty to learn. Noah and Will had shown her that.

Just then, the sounds of boots scuffing against dirt floated over her ears. Softly at first, then a little louder, they were coming from the south.

Sariah's ears perked up, and she fought against her inner excitement at being right. Sure enough, several men became visible moments later, walking up the road.

Their formation was odd. There were two walking in front, three in the middle, and two in the back—seven in all. The one in the middle looked a little different than the others. He carried no weapons and wore strange clothing. There were no chains on his hands or feet, so he likely wasn't a prisoner.

Royalty, maybe. It was hard to imagine a noble shacking up with awful people like the Dusk Ravens, but she really didn't know about their kind.

Most important, her magic had been dead-on. She

thought she'd sensed seven of them, and there they were. This night was getting better and better.

After what felt like hours of crouching and watching, the small group finally passed her to the north and were just outside her field of vision.

Not wanting to wait any longer, she started moving, going slowly to make sure they didn't see or hear her behind them.

Her legs ached, and the left one cramped a little from having sat in one position too long, but she pushed that from her mind so she could focus on following her quarry. She couldn't lose them now.

Several minutes later, the noise of boots on dirt lessened, then stopped completely. A slight chill ran up Sariah's spine, and she stopped, too.

She crouched low to the ground and tried to make as little noise as possible, but no one came her way. It seemed she was still unspotted, at least for now.

A cricket started making an awful racket off to her right. She desperately wanted to reach out and smush the thing to stop its incessant "cricket-cricket" noises. It was grating on her nerves, but she remained still. Crickets making noise were normal. Crickets suddenly stopping were strange. She couldn't let her targets suspect a thing, or the whole operation would be blown.

Up ahead, a bright light started to form at the edge of her field of vision. It was a small dot of light in an inky sea of blackness, but she knew what it was, a campfire. The Dusk Ravens were setting up camp.

Sariah let herself maneuver into a regular sitting position, and she breathed a sigh of relief. Enemies that set up camp right next to the road typically didn't suspect anything. Her little gambit had been successful so far.

The hardest part, of course, was still to come. She had to kill them all while leaving the secrets they carried intact and return those to Ilene and Will. All without getting hit herself.

Seven against one weren't great odds, but she had a plan to handle that. For now, all she had to do was wait it out a bit longer.

While she sat and waited for the light of the Dusk Ravens' fire to wane, her stomach grumbled. She looked down at her abdomen like it was betraying her.

"What? Now, of all times? Why now?" she whined at it in the quietest voice she could muster. It grumbled again in response.

Groaning, she rummaged in her pack for a ration. She had taken the time to liberate a few of the hard, rock-like things from the Talon's Reach larder before she'd left, and now she was glad she'd done so.

She took a bite of the ration and chewed it several times before swallowing. They didn't taste that great, but supposedly they had "everything a body would need to survive in the harshest conditions." That was another Will quote.

Sariah didn't know what bothered her more, that Will had a rule or a quote for just about everything, or that she'd memorized so many of them. Shrugging, she sighed and took another few bites of the ration.

If nothing else, at least it would calm her stomach down.

She thought about the alternative of sneaking up on the

Dusk Raven encampment, only to be brought down by her stomach's incessant rumbling. She didn't know whether to laugh or groan.

Before long, the light of the fire started to wither and eventually die down to nothing. Sariah smiled. Now was the time. Most of them would be asleep. With any luck, she'd have half of them dead before they even knew what hit them.

Sariah got up from her position and shook out her muscles. She rubbed the spot on her leg that had cramped earlier to relieve the tension. The last thing she needed was a debilitating cramp in the middle of the battle. Then she stuck the remaining uneaten half of her ration deep in her pack and secured it in place on her back.

She took a hesitant step forward. She wasn't quite sure her legs would respond after what felt like hours of being still. Fortunately, her feet obeyed her without question.

Nodding at her feet in appreciation, she took another step, then several more, moving as quietly as she could.

If the Dusk Ravens were smart, and there was no reason to believe otherwise, they'd have one or two guards keeping watch for people like her, so she had to remain quiet and careful.

She made her way along an inch at a time, or at least that's what it felt like until finally, she could make out the outlines of people in the distance. Sure enough, two of them were standing upright, though it looked like the rest of them were lying down.

It was hard to tell from this distance, so she crept forward just a little further to confirm her suspicions.

When she was perhaps fifty meters away, she could

make out all of their outlines. There were indeed five forms on the ground. Sariah let out a small sigh. So far, her plan had gone swimmingly. Now she just needed to bring it to its conclusion.

She reached into a sheath wrapped around her waist and pulled out several daggers. There were five in all. It was all she'd been able to scrape together from Talon's Reach without causing a scene.

That didn't leave her much room for second chances, but hopefully, she wouldn't need them. If she did, she would be in big trouble.

Sariah eyed the distance. With how dark it was, not even the moon was out tonight to light the way, she doubted her ability to make the daggers meet their intended targets with a standard throw.

Magic it was, then. This would be her first real magic test since the Battle of Chatwick.

She took a few deep breaths to calm herself and made a lifting motion with one of her hands. In response, two daggers rose up in front of her face. She stared at the blades for several moments in a trance-like state, then she pushed out with her hand and sent the daggers flying.

The first one hit its mark dead-on, landing deep in the neck of one of the Dusk Raven guards, killing him and cutting off his ability to warn the others in one fell swoop.

Unfortunately, the other dagger didn't fare as well. It sailed right past her intended target, landing somewhere well behind him with an audible thud.

The startled guard heard the noise and looked all about. He caught sight of the other guard sinking to the ground, and his expression changed to one of alarm.

"We're under attack!" he yelled. That was his last action, for a second later, another knife was sticking out of his neck as well. Sariah had taken advantage of his momentary confusion to ready another dagger and send it flying.

Two down, she thought. There were five left to go, and now she no longer had surprise on her side.

"Why must it always be the hard way?" she groaned. Then she sprang into action.

She ran the rest of the way to the encampment, intent on closing the distance before the remaining Dusk Ravens could mount a defense. When she reached them, three of the guards were up and reaching for weapons. The remaining guard and the oddly-dressed one remained on the ground.

Not wanting to waste the opportunity, she took her last two daggers and let them fly at the two Dusk Ravens still on the ground. If she took them out now, they wouldn't have a chance to sneak up on her later.

The first dagger met its mark in the guard on the ground's chest. She heard a slight gurgling noise, and he flailed around for a moment, then stopped. The second dagger clanked against some sort of metal around the oddly-dressed one's chest and fell to the ground, useless.

Damn it! He was armored!

There was nothing she could do about it now. She had three more armed guards to contend with first.

Sariah balled her hands and pushed toward the guard on her far left. A jet of flames poured from her fingertips, engulfing the unsuspecting Dusk Raven. He fell to the ground, writhing and screaming.

Four down. At least the odds were improving.

The remaining two guards seemed stunned by the sudden light of the fire engulfing their friend, so Sariah took full advantage, pulling out her sword and rushing at the one to the right of her.

She slammed into his abdomen head-first, forcing him to the ground in a tangled mess of gear and limbs. The guard tried to get up, but Sariah was on him before he could move, thrusting the blade of her sword deep into his chest with one quick motion.

The guard on the ground looked at the sword protruding from his body in shock for a moment, then his eyes went dark and he was gone. Sariah pulled on the sword to free it. It was stuck on something, but it came free soon enough.

A big sigh escaped her lips. She still had two more of these guys to take care of.

Her eyes darted around, quickly taking in the rest of the scene. There was one guard still standing, and the oddly-dressed one still on the ground. That one had his hands over his head like he was trying to block out the sights and sounds of death playing out around him.

Sariah tilted her head and gave him a quizzical look, then returned her gaze to the guard still standing. This guy had his sword out, and he looked ready to defend himself.

Even in this low light, Sariah could see the man knew what he was doing. He was holding his sword in both hands, and his feet were poised to let him both strike and defend with ease. This man was no ordinary Dusk Raven guard. He was a pro.

Ignoring the man on the ground for the moment, Sariah inched closer to the upright guard. The two of them circled each other, each feinting every now and then to taunt the other into acting.

After several moments of this, the Dusk Raven struck. He came in with a well-placed blow to Sariah's middle. She moved her own blade to intercept his with practiced ease.

"You're going to have to do better than that," Sariah taunted.

The Dusk Raven smiled at her. She could see he was missing a couple of teeth, so it was a bit of a ghoulish sight that put her slightly off guard.

Then he pounced on her again, coming in with a series of blows that pushed her back. She managed to deflect them, but only barely. Her attention hadn't been fully focused on the fight and had been on his oddly misshaped grin instead.

Keep your mind centered on the matter at hand, she heard Will's voice in her head. She groaned a little, but it was still good advice.

She lashed out with her blade and went for a couple of low strikes, which the Dusk Raven parried. She was starting to sweat and feel the cumulative effect of combat and magic. In that sense, she was outmatched as the Dusk Raven was still relatively fresh.

Undaunted, she made another wild strike at his middle. This one almost hit the mark, but he still blocked her.

He came at her again with a powerful thrust that sent her backward toward one of the fallen guards. She tumbled over his body and fell flat on her back.

The Dusk Raven cackled and raised his sword over his head to strike her down.

She closed her eyes and readied another jet of flame,

but before the man could move, she heard a howl and watched as a furry form overtook him.

Sariah got up off the ground and blinked a few times to take in the scene. It was Bear, her animal companion, his teeth gnashing as he raked her opponent's chest with his claws. The animal had come to her rescue, and just in time!

She didn't know how Bear even knew where she was.

It didn't matter. She could figure it out later.

"Bear!" she howled. "Get out of the way!"

The animal complied, rushing over to her feet. She readied a burst of flame, and it rushed forth, consuming what remained of her opponent.

Sariah beamed. Six dead Dusk Ravens lay at her feet. She reached down and scratched Bear behind the ears.

Something nagged at her. Where was the seventh member of the caravan?

As if on cue, she heard more than saw him running and screaming in the distance. For a moment, she considered sending Bear after him. He growled low in response, but she held onto him. The Dusk Raven had almost disappeared. He was too far away in the dark to follow.

"That's right!" she called after his fleeing form. "Go run home and tell your mommy on us!"

She smiled to herself, then looked at Bear and together, the two started to rummage through the dead bodies of her foes. She wanted to find this "technology" that they were carrying so she could bring it back to Talon's Reach.

Her search was interrupted by the sound of someone clapping.

"Not too shabby," a man's voice called to her.

Sariah's face turned into a scowl, and she looked in the

direction of the voice. "How nice to meet you all the way out here, Will," she replied. "Out for a stroll, I suppose?"

The hairs on the back of her neck tingled. Something was wrong. There was no way Will had just happened upon her like this. Her mind was racing. Had it all been a ruse? One thing she could be sure of. She did not like that he was out here one bit.

Will stepped into the light cast from the two dead bodies that were still burning. "Oh, you know, I thought I'd stretch my legs a bit. Get some fresh night air." He flashed her a smile. "Feels good on the skin, don't you think?"

"How about you? Taking your dog for a walk?" His eyes bulged slightly as he looked down at the animal, then back at her.

She shot him an icy glare and tilted her head to the side. "Why are you here? Really?" She suddenly felt more defensive in his presence than she had when up against the Dusk Ravens.

Will shrugged. "Well, when Ilene scuttled my plans to go after the Dusk Raven caravan, I figured I'd just do it myself." He looked at her. "But I see you've gone and done that for me."

He took a few more steps to close the distance between them. "The real question is, why are you out here at this hour? Who told you about this?"

A knot formed in her stomach, and she froze. She didn't know what answer she could give that wouldn't give it all away.

Will waved a hand dismissively. "It's okay. I know you were listening in on us the other night. You weren't that careful."

Sariah's cheeks felt hot. She drew in a deep breath to scream something but stopped herself short. "How did you know?"

"Your invisibility skills are pretty good, but it would do you well to remember that they don't muffle the sound. I heard someone skulking about loud and clear out there. I figured you were the only one with the gumption to do it."

Sariah gasped, and her jaw dropped open. After a moment, she nodded. "I suppose that makes sense." She straightened and looked him squarely in the eye. He still seemed angry about something. She decided to try changing the subject.

"Anyway, are you going to help me find this thing you were so intent on bringing back to Talon's Reach or not?"

Will shrugged and let out a short bark of a laugh. "Already did." He pointed at something behind Sariah. "He ran off thataway."

The blood drained from Sariah's face, and she stared wide-eyed at Will. "You don't mean…"

"Mmhmm." Will nodded. "That oddly-dressed guy was a magic user they were escorting to the Dusk Raven stronghold. Supposedly, the guy knows how to power these strange little devices called 'amphoralds.' But I guess now we'll never know for sure."

Sariah looked ashen. "Oh, Will, I'm so sorry. I had no idea." She clapped her hand over her mouth. "I guess it's a good thing I didn't kill him."

"Heh. Why is that?"

"Because now we have the chance to capture him again?" she said with a sheepish grin.

Will chuckled a bit. "Maybe." He looked down at the

carnage. "Well, maybe it won't all be for naught. Let's see if they had any correspondence of use, eh?"

Sariah nodded. "Sounds like a plan."

The two spent the next several minutes rifling through the pockets of the dead Dusk Ravens. All except the burnt two, of course. They were too burnt to have pockets left to search.

At first, it seemed like their search would turn up empty, but eventually, Sariah found something suspicious. It was a letter written on thick parchment, with a heavy wax seal on the back. Eagerly, she ripped off the seal and opened the letter.

Her eyes scanned the page's contents. It was hard to make out in the darkness, but soon she was able to focus on the tiny letters on the top fold of the page.

What she saw on the first few lines made her blood run cold. There at the top, in bright letters, were the words, "Gabriel, ruler of Stratton. I send my regards."

Sariah's heart skipped a beat. Her eyes darted around, looking for Will. He was hunched over another body and hadn't seen her yet.

Was it the same Gabriel she knew? Could he really have…

She shook her head. The missive had to be wrong. It just had to be. Slowly, she started to read further.

"What do you have there?" Will asked. He grabbed the document out of her hands before she could do anything.

"No, don't!" she protested, but it was too late. His eyes were greedily scanning the contents.

"This is a reply about a request for more troops to

guard Stratton. And it's addressed to the Dusk Raven general Gabriel!" Will cried.

Sariah sighed. "There has to be some mistake," she implored. "There just has to!"

Will's face turned bright red. "Are you really going to defend him? Now, of all times, after we took you in to help fight against him?" He looked at her with a look that was equal parts shame and disgust. "I knew your tale was too good to be true."

She blushed and hid her face. "No. No, that's not it at all," she insisted. "It's just…"

"Just what?" Will demanded.

Sariah lowered her head further. "Just nothing."

Will nodded. "I thought so." He reached out a hand to her. "Come, we must inform Ilene at once. Something must be done to save Stratton from the Dusk Ravens!"

Sariah looked up at Will's hand with surprise. She'd just practically committed treason, both by running off and then defending a criminal. Yet, Will was offering her a place next to him.

Had she been wrong about Will this whole time? It was hard to know for sure, but she was starting to see him in a new light.

She didn't think long on his offer. It was the best bet she had going for her, and Stratton deserved better than to wither under Dusk Raven control, even if it was Gabe at the helm. The people of Stratton were good, hard-working souls. She'd met several of them.

Sariah nodded and took his hand. "Lead the way."

CHAPTER FOURTEEN

When Harvey woke up, it was in a warm bed in his own home, not in the dust outside the Chatwick mine. He blinked a few times and shot up out of bed with a start.

He felt his side. There was a fresh bandage there, and only a slight twinge of pain. He smiled slightly. Whoever had cared for his wound had done a good job of it.

At the foot of his bed was Padron, sitting in a chair with a worried expression on his face. The room was empty other than him. "About time ya woke up, lad!" he said. "We was getting worried about ya."

Seeing Padron looking as healthy as ever set Harvey's mind at ease. "How long was I out?" he asked.

Padron shrugged. "A day or so. Not too long. Don't ye worry, we saved ya a piece of tha celebration cake." The rearick winked as he said the last word.

Harvey furrowed his brow. "Celebration cake?" The events of the previous day washed over him, and he remembered the escape and the ensuing battle.

"How many…"

The rearick shook his head. "None of us. Yer plan was a solid one, lad. We all made it out of tha mine safe an' sound, save old Comfry."

Harvey's chest tightened again at the thought of Comfry's sacrifice, but he pushed the thought aside. There were more important things to focus on. "How is everything in town? Are all the Dusk Ravens dead?"

Padron nodded. "Aye, lad. Those guards with Jeffrey were tha last of tha lot. We spent part o' yesterday sniffin' around town, but no one else is left. Just us regular folk."

Harvey breathed a sigh of relief. "That's good to hear. Were you able to find anything of use in the complex outside the mine?"

His rearick companion shrugged. "Just some discarded weapons and a whole heap o' amphoralds. Seems we were able to stop them from makin' a mighty big shipment to their home base. That ought to cheer ya right up."

"It does," Harvey admitted. He liked the thought that he'd set the Dusk Ravens' plans back, if only a little bit. They'd caused him and Sariah enough grief.

That only left one problem to deal with—how to reach Sariah. Once more, he cursed his lack of talent with mental magic. If only he could use it, he could have found her before this whole mess at the mine.

He wondered how she was doing and if she'd found the help she wanted.

A knock came at the door, interrupting his thoughts.

"Come in," Harvey said. He checked to make sure he was dressed and was relieved to see that he was.

"Sorry ta bother ya, chief," a female voice called from

the doorway. It was Justine. She walked into the room. "I hope ya got some good sleep after all that."

Harvey waved a hand at her. "It's no problem. What can I do for you?"

Justine's eyes traveled downward, then back up to meet his. Her cheeks flushed a bit. "Plenty, I'm sure," she said with a wink.

Is she hitting on me again? Harvey marveled.

The female rearick continued before he could ponder the matter any further. "Tis a small thing, chief, but tha villagers are kind of wonderin' what ta do next."

Harvey furrowed his brow again. "About what?" And why are they asking me? he added silently.

"About tha mine, o' course. That and tha amphoralds, tha dead Dusk Raven that was masqueradin' as tha foreman fer years, tha whole lot of it. It seems they need a leader, chief."

"They want me to tell them what to do?" Harvey blushed. "I'm no leader. I just did what was right."

Justine shrugged. "I s'pose yer right, but that don't stop them from thinkin' it, now do it?"

Harvey nodded. "I guess you have a point." He threw up his hands in defeat. "Well, anyone got any ideas?"

Justine took a half a step forward. "Actually, sir, yeah I do. I know a group of people that could really use those jewels. They're a few days' march north of here holed up in an old castle. The Eagle's Claw. You could say they're an enemy o' the Dusk Ravens if ya like."

Harvey blinked a few times. "How do you know all this?"

Justine shrugged again. "Cause I work fer 'em."

Harvey did a double-take. He couldn't believe it. First, the mine foreman had secretly been a Dusk Raven this whole time, and now an agent of their sworn enemy had also lived here secretly for years? It was too much to be a coincidence.

Maybe this group would know what had happened to Sariah. She had been looking for such a group when she'd left. Perhaps they could help him find her.

The corners of Harvey's lips curled upward into a big smile. "I'm listening."

"Absolutely not!" Ilene shouted in disgust.

Will pulled on his face. He took a step forward toward Ilene and away from Sariah, who had been standing by his side. The two of them had come to tell her of the impending danger to Stratton.

"Come now, my lady! We have to try something!" he implored.

Ilene crossed her arms. "The answer is no. We are not ready for that kind of conflict."

Will leaned in close to her and lowered his voice. "It was my idea, not Sariah's if that means anything," he offered.

Ilene glared at him. "Like that's supposed to mean something to me?" She rolled her eyes. "I trust your council on most matters, Sir William, and I'm willing to overlook your recent dalliance that brought us this information." She was scowling as she spoke. "But this is too much too fast."

Will's face turned bright red, and he balked at her. He threw up his hands in exasperation. "And what about the Dusk Ravens? If they get a hold of the full resources of Stratton? With resources like those at their disposal, they'll be unstoppable. What then?"

Ilene looked thoughtful for a moment. She placed a finger on her chin and looked upward, then returned her gaze to meet Will's. "I am sorry. The answer is still no. It would be like sending lambs to the slaughter to send our forces against the Dusk Ravens at this juncture. We need more time."

"I'm telling you, my lady, we don't have more time!"

Ilene looked away. "My answer stands. Now please, leave me in peace."

Will wagged a finger at her and opened his mouth as if to say something, then closed it. He turned to face Sariah. "Come, let's go."

"But what about—" Sariah started.

Will shrugged. "If she says no, then it's no."

"But—" Sariah repeated.

"There's no use fighting it," Will told her. "We might as well go."

He could tell from the fire in her eyes that Sariah wanted to stay and argue the point further, but he knew better. So he did the only thing he could think of and dragged her out of there by the arm.

"Hey!" Sariah yelled at him, trying in vain to free her arm. "You don't need to be so rough about it!"

Will chuckled. "You think that was rough? You have much to learn about rough things," he said with a slight raise of an eyebrow. They were out of the courtyard, and he was willing to drop the formalities.

"Oh bugger off!" she exclaimed, finally wrestling her arm free and pushing him away from her. "You men are all the same when it comes down to it."

Will shrugged again. He leveled a wry smile at her. "Maybe. But I'm still right."

Sariah rolled her eyes. "Enough banter. What are we going to do now? Stratton is in serious trouble if that missive is to be believed."

His eyes scanned the area for prying eyes or ears. Finding none, he leaned in closer to Sariah and spoke in a voice barely over a whisper. "Don't worry. I have a plan."

The girl looked into his eyes, searching for something but not finding it. At that moment, he really wanted to know what she was thinking. He didn't have to wait long.

Sariah straightened up and put her hands on her hips. "Yeah, well it better be better than the last one."

Gabriel got up from his bed and stretched. He was staying at The Dragonfly. He'd always liked their beds, and Evelyn had a decent spy network set up already that he could lean on for information, so it was convenient as well.

He scratched a spot on his back that had been bugging him for the past half hour, keeping him from sleeping in like he'd wanted to. The spot had eluded him, so he ended up using a hard bit of the wall as a scratching post. It did the trick well enough for now, at least.

His eyes took in his surroundings. The sun had risen

recently, and it was barely peeking into his room through the open window.

It was early yet. Not that it mattered that much. While he hadn't been in Stratton long, so far the days had gone pretty much the same. He started with a survey of the guards patrolling the town, then he picked a few "volunteers" to send off to the Master, then lunch, then mostly pointless waiting around.

Strangely enough, running a town wasn't nearly as hard or involved as he'd thought it would be. Of course, most of the town guards and officials had already allied themselves with the Dusk Ravens, so in reality, his "coup" hadn't taken much effort.

Which was a good thing because there weren't that many troops left from Severin's operation to work with. There were maybe a hundred tops and, at any given moment, a dozen of those were escorting villagers to the Dusk Raven stronghold nearby.

If anyone did manage to attack the town, he mused, they'd have a decent shot at coming out on top. Assuming they had a decently-sized force, of course. But who would be stupid enough to attack a walled city defended by the Dusk Ravens? Certainly not any group he was aware of.

So he spent most of his days sitting in his room or in a tavern somewhere, waiting for word from the Master that his occupation could come to an end, and thinking.

His thoughts were centered on Sariah. He still missed her dearly. He was positive that he could make up with her if only he could see her once again. But, truth be told, he wasn't even sure she was still alive.

He'd left her broken and bleeding outside his cabin,

with no one in range to help or heal her. Had she even lived? It was too much to think about, so he pushed the thought from his mind. She was alive. She had to be.

Where are you, Sariah? he asked himself. What are you doing right now?

Gabriel didn't have long to ponder, though. His thoughts were interrupted by the noise of a town guard busting through the door to his room.

It was one of the front gate guards, Sergeant Ty. He'd always kind of liked Sergeant Ty, though this morning, in particular, he was irate at the intrusion.

The guard had a fresh layer of sweat covering his face, and he was huffing and puffing like he'd run several blocks.

Gabe scowled at the man. He had half a mind to kill him right then for interrupting his alone time, but he stopped short. If the guard were here, it must be for something important.

"Yes?" he said in a low, grumbling tone.

"Master Gabriel! You must come quick! There are raiders at the front gate!" Ty managed through several labored breaths.

Gabe shot up. "Raiders?" he repeated, raising his eyebrows in consternation.

Ty nodded. "Aye, Master. Hundreds of them. Come quick!"

Gabe shook his head to clear the haze he'd been in. So there was someone stupid enough to attack them, after all.

His lips curled into a deep frown, and his fists clenched so tightly he practically drew blood from his palms.

Well, if they want a fight so bad, then they'll get one.

Harvey kept walking along the pathway. He was traveling with Padron, Justine, and a handful of the miners from Chatwick.

The miners had come along to help carry the load of amphoralds, which they'd brought at Justine's urging.

Justine had recently informed him that their destination wasn't much farther ahead. He supposed he had no real reason to doubt her. She seemed like an honest type, even if she had hidden her real allegiance for years.

Still, if she was leading them to their doom, he supposed he'd find out soon enough. He didn't think that was the case, though.

"Where is this dander-blasted town of yers?" Padron asked Justine. He had been growing more restless and upset over the past hours of marching.

Not that Harvey could figure out why. Padron traveled plenty on his own, and they were keeping a fairly even pace.

"Simmer down, Padron," Justine fired back. "Ye'll see it soon enough."

"Humph."

Moments later, the outline of some old, stone buildings became visible on the horizon. They slowly took the shape of a massive castle, one much larger than Harvey had ever imagined could be built.

Was this one of the wonders of the old race? he wondered, mouth agape. Out of the corner of his eye, he could see Padron and the others had similar expressions.

"That it?" Padron said, pointing toward the castle. He shrugged. "I expected bigger."

"Isn't that what all tha ladies say to ya, ya old coot?" Justine ribbed him.

Padron's face boiled with rage, and he wagged a finger at her, but in the end, he said nothing. Then all of them burst out laughing at once.

"Let's just get going," Harvey suggested once they had calmed down.

"Aye," Padron agreed with a nod.

The group made their way in silence until they were a stone's throw away from a giant door that barred their entry. Off to the side of the door stood a small structure that looked like a guard post.

"Oy!" Justine yelled. "Lester! Open tha gates an' let me in!"

Harvey heard a grumbling noise from the direction of the guard post, and then the sound of feet shuffling on stone. A moment later, an old man poked his head out of a small window. He looked disheveled, with more than a days' worth of stubble on his chin and wisps of white hair pouring out of his helmet at odd angles.

"What's that, now?" Lester asked. "Who goes there?"

Justine's face brightened a little. "'Tis me, ya old badger! Now let me an' me merry band 'ere through tha doorway!"

Lester rubbed his eyes, then blinked. "Justine? Is that you?" He looked the rearick up and down. "Why, you were much younger when I saw you last. Didn't think you were ever going to come back this way."

Justine rolled her eyes and tapped her foot. "Just let us in, already, old man!"

"Wait," Lester replied. "What's the password?"

"Password?" Justine said, exasperated. "Ye don't need no stinkin' password, ya old coot! Don't make me go an' get Ilene!"

That seemed to get a reaction out of the old gate guard. He nodded once and held out a hand. "Now you just wait patiently a minute. There's no need to involve Ilene in this. I'm opening the door, it just takes a minute," Lester explained.

"Uh-huh," Justine replied. She shook her head and let out a sigh.

Moments later, an ancient mechanism roared to life, and the massive door that stood in their way lowered into the ground. Harvey was glad they were as far away as they were, for the door came almost to his feet.

Justine motioned for the group to go with her into the castle, and they all complied. Harvey waited for everyone else to go first, then he followed.

Once they were inside, Lester walked out of the guard post to greet them properly. He looked even older face to face. Harvey wondered how he'd even stayed together as long as he had.

He turned to Lester and looked him in the eye. "Tell me, old man," he started. "Has a young girl named Sariah come through these parts?" There was a heavy note of pleading in his tone.

The old man looked up at him. He rubbed his chin for a moment before saying anything. At last, he nodded.

"Aye, that there was," Lester replied. Then he hung his head low. "Only you're a little late. She up and left not two days ago. Said there was someone she had to meet up north. Some guy named Gerbil."

Harvey frowned. Gerbil? He'd never heard of anyone by that name. Still, if Sariah had been here recently, maybe it wasn't too late to catch up with her.

A grim thought hit him, then. "Wait a second," he said. "Could it have been Gabriel?"

Lester rubbed his chin again. "Yes, I suppose that could have been it. Said she had to go meet him up in Stratton."

Harvey's mind raced. Sariah had found what she'd been looking for, a lead to Gabriel's whereabouts. Like a moth to a big, bright, dangerous flame, it was leading her right back up to Stratton.

His stomach churned as he turned the information over in his mind. In that instant, somehow, he knew that she was in trouble, and she needed help. Once again, he was nowhere close to her.

A single word escaped his lips. "*Scheisse!*"

CHAPTER FIFTEEN

Sariah, standing next to Will, looked over the field in front of her. They were standing tall and brave outside Stratton, not an hour past sunrise.

Bear nipped at her heels. The animal was tense and ready for battle.

"Easy now, Bear," she whispered. "You'll get your fill soon enough." She gave him a pat on the head.

She clapped her hand over her mouth. Will had instructed her to remain quiet, and here she was, mere meters from a highly fortified enemy structure, being noisy.

Will looked down at her and flashed her a smile. He waved at her dismissively with one hand. "It's okay, you don't have to be that quiet," he whispered out of the corner of his mouth.

She looked up at him with a frown. "Then why did you tell me to be dead silent?" she quipped.

He shrugged. "So you wouldn't go making an awful racket and spoil things."

Sariah shoved his arm. It had practically no effect on him. "I am not that bad," she insisted.

"Remember that stealth attempt of yours a week ago?" he chided her. "Not that great, either."

She rolled her eyes and crossed her hands in front of her chest. "Whatever."

Sariah glanced back at the main gate of Stratton. It had seemed so welcoming the last time she'd been here, but that had been under very different circumstances. Now it looked like an impenetrable wall of doom hell-bent on keeping her out.

Which, she supposed, was precisely what it was.

A slight chill ran down her spine, and it wasn't from the autumn air. Autumn had just started to turn, and it was still quite warm.

She looked back at Will, who was smiling at something in the distance. She moved her own gaze to see what it was and found it quickly. A small contingent of Dusk Raven forces were piling out of the main gate.

This only made her worry that much more. Her stomach started to churn, and she thought for a moment that she'd lose the morning's rations, but they managed to stay put somehow. Her forehead started to sweat. She used a hand to wipe it off while keeping her vision glued to the assembled forces. There must have been a hundred of them.

Sariah leaned in a little closer to Will. Her voice creaked as she spoke in a tone barely over that of a whisper. "You sure this plan is going to work?"

Will shrugged and flashed her a grin. "Has to."

She breathed a sigh of relief and started to relax slightly.

"Otherwise, we're all dead," he finished.

Sariah rolled her eyes. He might be right, but he didn't have to say it like that, did he?

Gabe stared out the front gates of Stratton in disbelief. He blinked a couple of times to make sure it wasn't a grand illusion.

Outside the gates stood no fewer than three hundred soldiers, decked to the nines in the finest gear he'd ever seen. Every soldier had a sword and a spear, and burnished gold armor covered virtually every weak point. The sight was downright daunting.

Where the hell did they even come from? he wondered.

He strained his eyes to try and see any symbol or crest that would tell him who they were, but he couldn't make anything out. Not that there could really be any doubt. There was only one other faction on Irth that could muster something even close to a force of that size, the Eagle's Claw.

It had to be them, but recent reports had estimated their number at no more than around two hundred. And that was all told, not just their soldiers. They had to have gotten help, but from whom?

Gabe stroked his chin. There was no point in worrying about it now. He nodded once to Sergeant Ty. "Tell the guards to assemble outside the main gates. We fight today to protect the city."

Ty nodded. "Yes, sir. I will have them ready at once." The man scurried off to accomplish his mission.

Gabe looked at the opposing forces again and let out a deep sigh. His worst fears were coming to fruition.

How had things ended up like this, anyway?

The thought wouldn't do him any good. He had a battle to fight. A battle he was determined to win.

Harvey woke with a start. His back hurt in at least a hundred places from the poor sleep he'd gotten the night before.

Originally, he'd considered not even sleeping, but he knew he was going to need his strength if he were to help Sariah. Teleporting as much as he had was really draining his reserves, so, sleep it was, as restless and awful as it had been.

He scanned the area around him. He was alone, but that didn't bother him. There was plenty for the others to do at the Eagle's Claw base. He was needed out here, close to Sariah. He tried to reach out with his magic to find her, but it was in vain. He was no good at mental magic, and he knew it.

She had to be just up ahead. The city of Stratton was right over the next bend, and that had been her destination if Lester was to be believed.

He marched on sore feet and wished for at least the dozenth time that he'd thought to bring more food with him. Alas, he'd left in too much of a hurry to think about it, with little more than a glance at Padron, who'd given him a knowing smile.

Harvey wondered how the rearick was doing, integrating with the others. He hoped the older man was okay. There was no reason to think otherwise.

Overhead, the sun had started to peek over the horizon just as the sprawling city came into view. When it did, Harvey practically did a double-take.

Standing outside the wall was an army of literally hundreds. The assembled men, adorned in glowing gold armor, formed an imposing wall that blocked the way forward.

Was Sariah among them, or had she already been captured?

Harvey let out another sigh. It didn't matter. With grim determination, he kept marching.

Sariah bit her lip as she watched the army of Dusk Ravens begin to march toward them.

"It's an easy enough illusion to maintain," Will told her. "All we're doing is making it look like we have more troops than we do. Even little Misty over there is capable of maintaining it," he explained.

He pointed with his head toward a girl not far off to his left, who was concentrating and chanting strange words. Misty was one of the perhaps twenty soldiers and mages that had come, including Albert, Sean, and all of the other people she'd trained with.

When Will had explained to them that Sariah needed

their help, they'd been quick to offer it. Now they were all here, about to die because of her stubborn stupidity.

She looked up at him briefly and then back at the Dusk Raven troops. "And?" she asked. "I said this plan had to be better than the last one."

"This way they're intimidated, and we get the upper hand," Will replied matter-of-factly.

Sariah looked out at the amassed forces again. "They don't look very daunted," she said.

Will shrugged. "Relax. That's only the first part of the plan. Besides. It's working, isn't it?" He pointed in the Dusk Ravens' direction.

She followed the direction of his finger. Some of the troops had broken rank and were running straight at them, while a few others were retreating back into town.

Sariah could hardly believe her eyes. It was working.

A smile crept upon her lips. "Nice work," she admitted. "Now what?"

Will flashed her a big smile. "Now the fun starts."

Sergeant Tennyson led his battalion toward the enemy. Shockingly, the enemy didn't move. It felt like they didn't even blink, they were so still. It was a little unnerving, but he was a seasoned pro. He wouldn't let such things get to him.

"Hold rank!" he called to his troops, hoping it would calm their nerves. If the enemy forces were putting him on edge, he could only imagine what it was doing to the others.

To his right, he noticed another battalion break rank and start running toward the enemy. He shook his head and yelled at them, but it was no use. That group's commander didn't seem to have the discipline that he did and was powerless to stop his troops from devolving into a mob.

"Hold rank!" he demanded again. His troops, restless as they seemed, obeyed his command.

They kept marching. Soon, they'd make contact with the imposing force.

"Striker formation!" Tennyson shouted. His battalion shifted position slightly to take up their new positions. Tennyson nodded and noted to himself that his troops were holding up remarkably well. It gave him hope for the coming confrontation.

"Keep it up, men, and we'll all go back home to our families tonight," he reassured them. There were a few nods.

Just then, the group that had broken rank ran into the enemy line. Literally, they ran straight through them like they weren't even there.

Sergeant Tennyson narrowed his eyes, thinking it a trick, but it wasn't. It was like the enemy troops didn't even exist.

All at once, it clicked. The enemy forces were nothing but an illusion! They were a trick meant to put the city guards on edge.

With this knowledge, he opened his mouth to shout new orders, but never got the chance.

At that same moment, the ground in front of them lifted straight into the air and came crashing down in his direction. He let out a wild death-wail as Irth itself fell on top of him.

***

Sariah watched as Will made a few odd motions with his hands. A huge slab of ground picked itself up in the air—with several soldiers still on it—and then slammed into the enemy troops, crushing them under its weight.

The big man was panting hard, but he remained standing.

She looked up at him with newfound respect. "You're going to have to teach me that trick when we get out of this!"

Will nodded. "If we get out of it, you mean." He pointed off to the right where several enemy troops were running about, slashing their weapons and looking confused.

"The ruse is up. They'll realize the truth soon enough. Then the real fighting begins."

Bear let out a yelp and crouched low to the ground, ready to pounce.

Sariah's lips curled into a smile. She brought her hands up, and a fireball started forming at the tips of her fingers.

Will pushed her fingers down and shook his head at her. "Save it," he insisted. "You'll need your strength for later."

She frowned but nodded. "Okay."

"Besides," he added. "Noah filled me in on your magic prowess. Not exactly the best."

Sariah shoved him, and in his slightly weakened state, he almost fell over. "Hey!" she whined. "I'm not that bad."

He shrugged again. "If your sword work is anything to go by, you're not that great, either."

Gabe watched in horror as his vanguard got eaten alive by a wall of dirt. "Damn it!" he cursed. "They have mages!"

"Sergeant Ty!" he barked. But Ty was no longer by his side.

Gabe rolled his eyes and sighed. It was so hard to find competent men these days. He pulled his sword from his sheath and strode forward out of the gates.

Time to take matters into my own hands, he thought.

He caught sight of several soldiers running back toward the town and snorted in disgust. "Soldiers, to me!" he cried. They didn't listen and kept running. He shook his head.

Gabe looked at the enemy force and watched as they magically dissolved into nothing, leaving behind nothing but a rag-tag group of perhaps twenty in all at the center of it.

A wry smile crossed his lips, and he tightened his grip on his sword. He could take them all on, even without an army. This would be child's play.

Then, out of the corner of his eye, he caught an odd sight and swore again.

"Sariah!" he exclaimed. She'd come for him at last.

Will watched the illusion drop as Misty fell to the ground. She'd kept it up as long as she could. He went over to the girl and laid her out on the ground, then stood over her. That girl had helped give them a chance. Will intended to make sure she lived to hear about it.

All around him, the enemy started to close in. He gritted his teeth. This was the hard part.

"Sean! Albert!" he called. Two young men looked in his direction. "Give us some cover fire. Thin out their numbers." They nodded and went to work.

"Trevor! Bindi!" he shouted toward two others. They looked at him as well. "Cover us on the other side." They nodded.

"Everyone else, get close. This is about to get messy."

He tightened the grip on his sword as he watched the enemy start to press in. They were still outnumbered. Even with the magical assistance from his fledgling mages, there would still be two to one or worse odds by the time the real fighting started.

In the corner of his eye, he could see massive fireballs being thrown by his men. Most of them managed to impact at least one enemy combatant, though a few went wide and did nothing.

Will let them pepper the enemy troops for a moment longer, then he called off their attacks. He didn't want them sapping all their strength just yet.

Just then, one of the Dusk Ravens broke rank and ran straight for him. With practiced ease, Will severed the man's head from his body, barely breaking a sweat in the process.

He grinned at the remaining forces, practically begging them to come at him.

Now for the really fun part.

Sariah struck out with her blade, slicing into one of the Dusk Ravens that had advanced on her. Where he had been, another one took his place.

In front of her, she caught occasional glimpses of Bear rushing between the legs of enemy troops, severing a tendon here, or gnashing at a leg there.

But they just kept coming.

It seemed there was no end to them. The new Dusk Raven in front of her made a wild swipe at her middle, and she parried it with her own blade before turning it to the side and slicing upwards.

Her own blade met nothing but air, but the Dusk Raven was forced back ever so slightly.

Lunging forward, she impaled the soldier between the second and third ribs. It was a strike Will would be proud of, not that she was sure where he was. Rule twenty, she thought. Always aim for the vital organs when you can.

She quickly scanned her surroundings, but it was nothing but Dusk Raven brown and blood in every direction. She hoped he was okay. He'd put so much on the line for her. All of them had really.

Another Dusk Raven came at her then, this one better than the last. He swung at her with a few low strikes, which she managed to beat back but not well.

She lunged at him and managed to land a glancing blow, but nothing that would keep him down.

Just then, she heard the sound of someone calling her name.

Her blood chilled. It sounded like Gabe, but she couldn't quite tell.

The momentary distraction was all it took for the Dusk Raven assaulting her to get past her guard. He thrust forward, and she fell to the ground to dodge out of the way of his sword.

She saw the soldier smile as he adjusted his blade to go for a downward thrust and end her. She shielded her face with one hand and readied a fireball in the other.

Harvey watched in amazement as the massive force outside the city of Stratton dissolved into nothing, leaving only a few troops behind. Who they were, he couldn't quite make out, but he knew they were in trouble.

At the same time, he watched a throng of Dusk Raven soldiers perhaps eighty strong advance on the small band.

He didn't have long to think, so he vaulted into action, running as fast as he could to reach the stalwart group of defenders in the center of the field.

After a few steps, it was clear he wasn't going to get to them in time to do much. The Dusk Ravens would reach them first. He could only hope he was fast enough to still make a difference.

Harvey ran so fast he practically didn't even see the ground, keeping his attention focused on the small band of soldiers now engaging head-on with the Dusk Ravens. He spotted several men of varying sizes and a few women, including one rather petite one on the outer rim.

His heart lurched, and his stomach churned. The small girl was Sariah!

I'm not too late! he thought. At least, not yet.

As he watched the battle unfold, he saw Sariah fall to the ground under the onslaught of a Dusk Raven.

Thinking fast, he summoned forth a fireball and sent it careening into Sariah's attacker. The man flew backward from the impact, taking a few other Dusk Ravens with him in a writhing ball of flame.

"Sariah!" he called as he closed the last bit of distance between them. He stood over her and offered a hand.

She took it readily and stood next to him. "Harvey!" she cried. "Aren't you a sight for sore eyes!"

He flashed her a dopey grin. "Oh, you know me, couldn't keep away."

Sariah pointed to something behind him. "Yeah, well, there's still more incoming."

Harvey turned to see a fresh set of Dusk Raven soldiers. He nodded. "Right. Let's show them who's boss."

Before he could do anything else, he heard the familiar and somewhat sickening sound of someone calling Sariah's name.

His blood practically boiled in his veins. It was Gabriel. That snake was here, and he was searching for her.

Harvey balled his fists and clenched his teeth, then looked over at Sariah. From her expression, it was clear she'd heard it, too.

"Gabe is looking for me," she said to him.

"I heard." He looked at her and shrugged. "Well, let's go get him, then."

Sariah smiled back at him. "Wait!" she cried. She was looking around for someone.

Out of the corner of his eye, Harvey saw a big man, bigger than him, though much leaner, edge toward them.

"Go," Will said with a half-smile. "We'll clean up the rest."

"Thanks, Will!" Sariah shot back. She flashed him a grin of her own.

Harvey stared at the two of them for a moment, wondering what had gone on that he'd missed. Then Sariah was back at his side, and all was right with the world. All save the Dusk Raven soldiers crushing in around them.

Sariah held out a hand to him. "Let's go."

Gabe looked out over the battlefield. Despite his superior numbers, his side seemed to be losing. It was unbelievable.

He'd have cared more about it, but they were all worthless in the long run anyway. The only one he cared about was Sariah. He spotted her again, standing next to that boy Harvey.

Gabe frowned. Somehow the boy had survived, too, and had come to help her. At their feet was Bear.

He scowled. So the dog came back, too. And still lapping at her heels. *Et tu*, Bear?

"Sariah!" he called again, louder this time. She turned her head slightly, so he knew she'd heard him, even though they were still far from each other.

Slowly, Sariah and Harvey made their way through the Dusk Ravens toward him.

Gabe scowled. I guess I'll have to take care of him first.

He watched as one of the Dusk Raven soldiers got a little too close to his beloved as they marched onward, oblivious. With a slight twitch of his fingers, he summoned forth a blast of energy to knock the Dusk Raven out of the way.

The soldier's body flew several feet and landed with a crunch, broken and bleeding on the ground, but Gabe didn't care. None of them mattered.

Only Sariah mattered. He would have his chance to talk to her at last.

The two of them were getting closer. "Sariah!" he shouted over the din of battle. "You've come home at last!" He smiled as he spoke the last words.

That smile was soon wiped from his face when Sariah lifted her hands and threw a fireball at him.

He deflected the blast easily enough, but the message was loud and clear. She had come for him, yes, but not to reconcile. No, she had come to kill him.

The corners of his lips curled downward into a snarl and his eyes filled with rage. He should have expected as much. "Fine!" he spat. "Have it your way!" Then he turned and ran back into the town.

CHAPTER SIXTEEN

Sariah watched Gabriel turn and run back into the town with a look of confusion on her face. "That coward!" she spat at him.

Harvey nodded in agreement. Bear let out a loud bark. "Come on," he said. "Let's go after him."

"Agreed."

With that, the three ran after Gabe, the battle raging outside the gates of the city momentarily forgotten.

Sariah hoped that Will and the others would manage without her. The enemy numbers had already been whittled down considerably by the time Gabe had appeared, so she was pretty sure they'd be okay.

Besides, she needed to confront Gabe if they were to win. Somehow, deep down, she knew he wouldn't stop unless she took care of him personally. And while Will was strong, he was also winded, and Gabe was stronger.

She ran through the streets of Stratton with Harvey at her side and Bear in front, chasing after their quarry.

The streets of the city were remarkably empty at this hour of the morning. Which was just as well. She didn't want any civilian casualties if she could avoid it.

Up ahead, she caught a slight glimpse of Gabe's shirt to the left. She summoned another fireball and let it fly, but it went into the side of a house instead.

The house sparked into flame, and Sariah let out a slight yelp. Her mind raced, trying to come up with an answer.

Noah's teachings sprang to mind. She'd put out fires in training before. She could do it here, too.

With trembling fingers, she conjured a sheet of ice over the burning wood, putting out the flames before they could cause any damage.

Sariah wiped a bead of sweat from her brow and let out a small sigh of relief.

"Come out and face me like a man, Gabriel!" she shouted after his fleeing form.

"What's the matter, afraid of a little competition?" Harvey added.

It was no use. Gabe didn't stop running.

Sariah gritted her teeth and kept going.

Gabe rounded another corner and felt the heat of flames at his back. He spared a glance to make sure his clothes weren't on fire. One of the seams was a tad singed, but that was it. He whistled in relief. That one was too damn close for comfort.

His gaze returned to the path in front of him. He was

almost to where he wanted to be. Up ahead, not too far along the path, was a clearing. He could lie in ambush there and take out Harvey. Then Sariah would be all his.

He was still confident he could win her over if only he could talk to her one on one like he wanted.

"You'll have to do better than that!" he shouted over his back as he kept running. He felt like a fool running away but reminded himself it was only temporary. Soon, he'd have the advantage. Then nothing would stop him. He'd have what he sought even if half the city had to die first.

He took another couple of turns and almost ran into a merchant head-first in the process. The poor fool looked confused and alarmed.

Gabe pushed the merchant face-down into the ground, figuring it would serve as a good distraction for Sariah and Harvey, then kept onward. He was meters from his goal now.

A few twists and turns later, and he was there at a decently sized clearing in the mess of buildings in this part of town. Just up ahead was the alcove where he could wait for Harvey and Sariah to come to him.

He thought about taunting them to come closer but figured that would spoil half the fun. So instead, he found a quiet corner and lay in wait.

Moments later, Harvey, Bear, and Sariah came across the merchant that Gabe had pushed into the ground. Sariah stopped briefly to help him, much to Harvey's chagrin.

"This was probably all part of his plan to escape!" he insisted. Even Bear nodded and let out a yelp.

"I can't help it," Sariah shot back. "I don't care if it's part of his plan. We're better than him. We have to help!"

Harvey had to admit she was right. "Fine, just be quick about it!" He tapped his foot for a minute, then he ended up going over and helping the merchant get his things together just to speed her up.

They kept going after that and came upon a precarious corner, not much further down the road. It looked like there was a bit of an opening up ahead around the corner.

Harvey's blood froze. He looked over at Sariah. She looked spooked, too.

"Come out from hiding and let's talk!" Sariah shouted into the air.

Harvey rolled his eyes at her. Lines like that weren't going to be successful. "I sincerely doubt he's in a talking mood right now," he quipped.

Sariah looked ahead of them. "Let's just keep going," she offered.

Harvey nodded. He took a few steps forward, but Sariah put out a hand to stop him.

"Wait!" she whispered. "Something's not right."

Harvey looked at her critically. "I get it," he replied. "Gabe's just up ahead, waiting for us." It was more of a statement than a question. "Isn't he?"

Sariah inclined her head and kept staring.

"Come on out, you coward!" Harvey yelled into the alleyway ahead of them. There was no response.

He started forward again, but Sariah still held him back.

"There's a trap up ahead," she told him.

"Of course, there's a trap!" he snapped.

But his thoughts were racing. Yes, there would be a trap waiting for them. Undoubtedly a deadly one. Gabe was up ahead, intent on killing him and probably Sariah, too.

Sariah was just brash enough to spring it and endanger herself. He frowned. He needed to spring it instead. It was the only way to ensure she made it out alive.

Finally, he thought. Finally, I'll have my chance to protect her.

He flashed her a dopey grin, one so big it strained his cheeks, and waved a hand at her dismissively. "Of course, it's a trap," he repeated coolly. "And unlike the last several times, this time I can spring it for you."

Before either she or Bear could stop him, he darted forward.

"Wait!" Sariah cried. It was too late. Harvey had run into the clearing without her.

Bear took off at once, intent on stopping him, but Harvey was too fast this time.

She ran forward as fast as her feet could carry her, her heart racing. What would she do if Harvey got hurt in her stead? Her whole reason for leaving him behind had been to protect him. She couldn't even imagine it.

Rounding the final bend, she spilled out into a large clearing. In front of her was Harvey, arms raised, glaring at Gabriel. Bear was in between them, crouched low and baring his fangs.

Gabriel's hands moved faster than sight, and a massive

fireball careened toward Harvey, who threw himself onto the ground, trying to dodge out of the way.

"Harvey!" Sariah squealed. She was too late. She looked down at her friend. He was still breathing, but his back was singed, and he'd been hurt badly at the very least. Bear lay next to him, not looking much better. At least both were still breathing.

A tear formed in her eye as she looked at them lying injured. It was all her fault.

"Sariah," Gabe said then in a casual tone, breaking her out of her trance. "How nice of you to join us."

Harvey coughed a few times and got up to a kneeling position at the same moment. A fireball formed in his palm and shot toward Gabriel, but the older man batted it away like it was nothing.

"Just in time, too," Gabe added. There was an intense fire in his eyes. His lips curled upward into an evil smile, and he raised his hands to strike again.

Sariah's eyes widened as she took in the scene. Her heart practically leaped out of her chest as she realized what was about to happen. Gabe was going to kill Harvey.

"No!" she screamed, reaching forward with her own force of will to shield her two companions just as a massive wall of blue energy swallowed them whole.

Sariah's eyes were blinded by the brilliant blue light for a moment, and she couldn't make out anything. Slowly her vision cleared. Beside her, she could barely make out the outline of Harvey still kneeling with Bear beside him, looking just like they had before the attack.

Gabe was standing with his hands still raised, and his mouth open in shock.

Somehow, she'd been successful. She'd protected Harvey and Bear from Gabe's wrath. A small sigh of relief escaped her lips, and she lowered her hands to her sides.

Harvey looked at her, then, his eyes wide. He said nothing, but nodded at her and beckoned for her to take a step toward their attacker. The message was clear, he'd let her talk to Gabe on her own, but he had her back if she needed it.

"How?" Gabe asked her, still in shock. "How did you do that?"

But the answer never came. Sariah lashed out at him with her own wave of energy, which he managed to block, but not as easily as before.

"How dare you!" she accused him. "After everything we've been through, you think I'd let you kill them right in front of me?" Her eyes carried their own fire now. "You think that would help win me to your side?"

Gabe held up his hands. "It wasn't like that. He was going to kill me first!"

Sariah pushed forward with a hand and sent another blast of energy toward him. "Yeah? Well, you deserved it! You set up this whole trap to try and kill him in the first place, and maybe take me with him!"

Gabe sighed. "No!" he insisted. "Never! I'd never hurt you!"

His eyes narrowed, then, and Sariah caught a slight movement of his. A wave of energy came at her, but she pushed out with her magic and blocked it much as she'd blocked Gabe's earlier attack.

Her eyes darkened further, and she shot more waves of energy at him as she continued advancing. Gabe, for his part, was still able to deflect the spells, but it looked like it was getting harder for him to do so.

"I thought you cared for me!" Sariah demanded.

"I do!" Gabe insisted. "You're all that I ever wanted!"

"Yeah, well, trying to kill Harvey and me is a pretty piss-poor way to show it!" She was only a few feet away from him.

Gabe put up his hands in mock defense. "Please, Sariah. Please, let's just talk it out. I was going to tell you the truth about everything, I swear. I just wanted you to be ready for it first."

Sariah cocked her head to the side. "You wanted me to be 'ready' for it?" He nodded. "For what, exactly? So you could tell me in person what a giant douchebag you are?"

She slammed him with another blast of energy. This one knocked him to his knees.

"No, of course not! I...I...just wanted you to like me!" Gabe told her. "Please, let's just stop all this nonsense. We can go somewhere and talk. Just the two of us. I'm sure you'll see it my way once we've had a chance to cool down."

His eyes had a wild, almost feral look to them. Then his face slackened and contorted into a weird smile that felt out of place. "I love you, Sariah."

Sariah stopped short. Of all the ways she'd imagined Gabe saying those words, and she'd imagined it plenty after their little date in Chatwick, this had to be the very last one.

She looked down at Gabriel on his knees, and her look changed from one of hatred to one of pity. She had come so far in the last month without him. She could see that now. And what did Gabe have to show for it, exactly?

Not much, she decided. If anything, he was even worse than before.

Gabe smiled up at her. "I knew you'd see it my way," he offered with a sly grin. "Come on, my darling, let's—"

Sariah pulled her arm back and decked him. He slumped to the ground, unconscious. "Just shut up already."

***

Harvey and Sariah sat down next to each other in the little clearing. Bear rested his head on Sariah's lap. The dog looked a little worse for wear, but he was sure the dog would make it out just fine.

About ten feet away, Gabe was sprawled out on the ground where Sariah had left him.

Harvey's whole back stung and felt like it was on fire from Gabe's attack, and he thought he was missing half an eyebrow, but otherwise, he was all right. A little rest and maybe a quick trip to a healer, and he'd be right as rain. It had all been worth it to protect Sariah, anyway.

The young man looked at Sariah, and he smiled. He had waited so long to see her again. Now that she was there and the danger was over for the moment, he had no idea what to say to her.

So instead, he put his arm around her. As he did so, she leaned against him, and they sat together for what seemed like an hour.

A sigh escaped Sariah's lips. He looked down at her and wondered what she was thinking.

She looked up at him, and their eyes locked together. In that moment, desire for her coursed through him stronger than it ever had before. He wanted her, more than he'd ever wanted anything in his entire life.

He looked deep into her eyes and saw a closeness and a sameness that hadn't been there before. It wasn't the same as his longing, but still pleasant.

I bet I could kiss her right now and she wouldn't stop me, he thought. What a joy that would be for both of them.

Alas, now was not the time. Not like this, with Gabe lying not ten feet away. She deserved better than that. Instead, he let out a sigh of his own and looked away.

He nodded in Gabe's direction. "So, what are you going to do with him?" he asked.

Sariah shrugged. "I don't know, honestly," she admitted. "Throw him in jail, maybe? If there's a jail strong enough to even hold him, that is."

Harvey let out a low whistle. "I don't think your new friends are going to be very happy with that plan."

She shrugged again. "I'm not going to give them much choice. Besides, it's not like I can kill him now. Not defenseless like he is. It wouldn't be right. Not even for Captain Dungbag."

"Captain Dungbag?" Harvey repeated with a gleam in his eye. "I'm sure he'll just love that nickname."

"It's not like I'm going to give him a choice about that, either." She flashed him an evil grin.

Harvey let out a hearty chuckle. "We'll need to do something with him. I get why you can't kill him, but I'm not sure anyone else is going to see it that way. That Will character didn't look like the understanding type."

Sariah nuzzled her head into his shoulder. "Let's just focus on something else for now, okay?"

He sighed but complied. They had a lot to catch up on. They could deal with Gabe when he woke up. "I met your friends in the Eagle's Claw, by the way," he said, changing the subject. "Well, the ones that stayed behind, at least."

Sariah's head bobbed up. "Oh?"

He smiled. "Yeah. They seem like nice folks."

She nodded at him. "They are. Well, most of them, anyway. That Will character is someone to watch out for."

"Yeah," he replied. He couldn't be sure, but he thought he detected a hint of longing or admiration when she spoke about Will. He thought about the tall, slender warrior he'd seen briefly outside Stratton. Standing with his sword in hand, he'd seemed imposing.

A small wave of jealousy washed over him, but he let it pass. He was with Sariah now. Will was not.

He took a moment to clear his head. "So, what's next?" he asked her. "For us, I mean. What's our next grand adventure?"

What crazy plan are you going to concoct this time? he added silently. She always got them into the stickiest of situations, but he was starting not to mind it. That was just a requirement of living with her.

"I still have an enemy out there," Sariah replied matter-of-factly. "The Master is still waiting for us. Somehow, I don't think he's going to take kindly to us defeating one of his armies."

Harvey nodded. That he could agree with. He tried to come up with something witty or some reason why she should slow down for a bit, maybe take a break, but there was nothing.

He settled for flashing her one of his signature dopey

grins. "Well then, we'll just have to get to him before he can get to us."

Sariah smiled lazily up at him, then nuzzled her head back under his shoulder. "Sounds like a good plan."

The Master is coming. He's going to kill Sariah, and all her friends. His power is terrifying and relentless.

Even with an army to protect her, does she really stand a chance?

Find out in *Triumph Through Magic*!

Grab your copy today at Amazon and Kindle Unlimited.

First of all, thank you so much for reading through this entire book, and for now reading these author notes! It means the world to me to be able to share these characters and this journey with you! If it weren't for you fans, I would never have become an author.

I'm really hoping you enjoyed this story. I know I did. Harvey really starts to come into his own as a character in this novel, and Sariah finally starts to grow up and realize maybe getting help from other people isn't such a bad thing. Plus she finally starts to learn some really kick-ass magic, and well, who doesn't love that?

This book was a hard one for me to write. Real-life complications got in the way when I was working on this manuscript. I got really sick for one, which killed my productivity for a few weeks, and my kids also had a lot of doctor appointments during this time. Way more than normal, but family comes first, so you do what you have to do as a dad.

So I ended up having to cram a lot of writing time into

a few short weeks to get this book back on track and meet my deadlines. That meant writing at least 10,000 words a week, and I only got time on the weekends to actually write, so my weekends were just as busy as my weekdays for a while.

But it was worth every single second in order to bring this lovely story to you, because I think it really does the characters justice. And it sets up the next book nicely.

It's hard to pick a favorite scene in this book for me. There are so many great moments to pick from. I loved the Harvey stealth scene. It was fun to write, and I enjoyed watching him grow from somewhat of Sariah's lap dog to a real threat in his own right. Plus there's just something about the tension in a stealth scene that makes it fun to read and write.

Another one of my favorites was Sariah's battle with Gabe at the end. I think I re-wrote the ending sequence three full times before it had the tone I wanted from it. I wanted Sariah to realize that she no longer had anything to prove herself for with Gabe, and that she didn't need his affection or approval anymore, and I think I finally managed to get that across. Even if she does still pine for him a little bit. But hey, first loves are hard to get over, am I right?

Then of course there was the death scene where Comfry sacrifices himself. I didn't even know who he was until I wrote that scene, but it still managed to hit me right in the feels. It was just the right amount of sad and awesome at the same time. Crazy, right?

What about you? What was your favorite scene? I'd love to hear all about it. Or even your least favorite scene, if you prefer. Drop me an email any time at peter@peterjglenn.com and tell me all about it. I absolutely adore hearing from my fans. Each little note from one of you is like a little present that I get to open and cherish. It's like birthdays or Christmas any time of the year, and it makes my whole day when someone says something nice about my works.

That's why I do this whole crazy career called writing in the first place - for you the fans! The long hours, the second guessing, the balancing twenty different things all at once, none of it would be worth anything if not for the love and attention I get from all of you.

If you liked this book, *please* leave a review. It really does mean the world to me. My wife can tell you, I rave about every single review I get to her and just about anyone else that will listen (as of this writing, I've gotten 11 total, and they all rock. I'd love to get a dozen more!)

Plus, a bunch of good reviews *might* just help that next book come out that much faster. There's still loads of adventures for Sariah left in my head just waiting to get put down on paper. Not to mention all the other characters that want their turn in the spotlight! Harvey needs a new opponent!

Loved the book a lot? Give me a follow on social media, too: www.facebook.com/authorpeterglenn OR join my mailing list: www.peterjglenn.com/email. Or heck, do both! The more the merrier! I also have giveaways and exclusive behind the scenes info on my mailing list, so join up!

I'd love to get a shout out from you in either spot and hear about what you'd like to see in an upcoming Sariah

Chronicles adventure. Who knows? Maybe I'll even name a future character after you (if you ask nicely, of course).

Thank you again for joining me on this journey and sticking with it until the very end, and I do hope you'll join with me again in future books.

Auf Wiedersehen.

Over the last few days, I've been able to enjoy some time with my parents who flew into town. It has been a while (not including a funeral last year) that we have spent any time with them, but I felt like…

It hadn't been much time at all.

With Zoom, phone and text, it just feels like they have been down the street and I just didn't go over to their house.

Mind you, they really live in Brenham, Tx (Go Bluebell Ice cream!) and I live in Las Vegas, so not easy to make the trip so fortunately I have a better excuse than simply lazy.

Oh, and COVID.

I enjoy watching new authors go through their early book releases and vicariously get to remember what 'the beginning' is like all over again. Peter was on Slack the other day hyped over a fan that reached out to him on his website.

I like to allow my mind to wonder how many thousands of times a day, the internet has allowed fans such as you to reach out and make an author's day just by saying 'I enjoyed the book.'

As a pulp writer, I'm into the stories and the characters. I have no hang-ups that I'm writing literary fiction, but I've had enough fans mention to me that my stories, or those of my collaborators helped them through tough times. Whether that is sickness, death of a loved one, COVID or whatever.

So, whether anyone ever recognizes the benefit those of us who write provide for our fans from an awards focus, you readers are the best. You let us know we help, you encourage our efforts to continue and you are the reason we get to do what we love.

So, *thank you.*

Without fans such as you – we don't get to write about crazy characters and their crazier antics and get them out of our minds. Perhaps *now,* some of them will stay quiet enough to let me sleep.

Ad Aeternitatem,

Michael Anderle

CONNECT WITH THE AUTHORS

Peter Glenn Social

Website: www.peterjglenn.com

Email list: www.peterjglenn.com/email

Facebook:
www.facebook.com/authorpeterglenn

Michael Anderle Social

Website: http://lmbpn.com

Email List: http://lmbpn.com/email/

Facebook:
https://www.facebook.com/LMBPNPublishing